THE FORTY DAYS

A VISION OF CHRIST'S LOST WEEKS

D1521680

D. MICHAEL MacKINNON

A POST HILL PRESS BOOK
ISBN: 978-1-68261-063-3
ISBN (eBook): 978-1-68261-064-0

THE FORTY DAYS
A Vision of Christ's Lost Weeks
© 2016 by D. Michael MacKinnon
All Rights Reserved

Cover Design by Christian Bentulan

Post Hill Press
275 Madison Avenue, 14th Floor
New York, NY 10016
posthillpress.com

EDITOR'S NOTE:

When he was but a boy of five years of age existing in squalor, crippling dysfunction, and repeated homelessness, the author was touched and comforted by the "Baby Jesus" from a small plastic Nativity scene. Since that moment, his faith and belief have only grown over time.

Years later as an adult, the author often had momentary flashes in his mind regarding The Forty Days after the Resurrection when Jesus walked the earth. The primary message always being: "There is a very special story attached to that miraculous time. Tell it." But even with those quick flashes of thought, he had no idea how to write such a story. Over the next number of years, the thoughts and flashes continued but with no blueprint. Then, in but a few short minutes during one day in August of 2015, the entire book, including character names and story, flooded into the author's mind. To this day, the author has no idea how or why it happened.

As it was happening and after, the author transcribed the thoughts from his mind as fast as possible onto paper and then wrote the entire book in basically one sitting. Still not entirely sure what was happening or what to do, the author reached out to a number of people in publishing. While all were instantly excited or intrigued, some wanted the author to change the story to make it more "commercial" and "exciting."

The author flat-out refused.

He strongly believed that it was imperative that the story be told *exactly* as it had flooded into his mind on that special day.

We agreed.

What follows is that simple, moving, and faith-affirming story *exactly* as it came into the mind of the author.

For any and all Christians on this earth now being persecuted, tortured, or killed because of their faith and because of their belief in Jesus Christ.

CHAPTER ONE

"I saw him. I touched him. I followed him."

Leah looked lovingly at her grandfather as his seventy-nine year-old eyes glowed with a light and an excitement she had never seen before.

"You saw who, grandfather?"

The old man sat at a crude wooden table in a corner of the small one room stone, mud, and straw home as his granddaughter and her husband Benjamin sat at the other end. Behind them, near the far wall, lying atop a thin blanket and a bed of hay, slept the couple's two young children.

The old man gazed at his great-grandchildren with pure love, pride...and something else. He looked upon their innocent faces for several seconds and seemed to gather strength from the act.

He then shifted his dark and weary eyes back to the young woman who was sitting across from him while she cleaned vegetables in a bowl before her.

"I kept it a secret all these years. I was afraid to tell anyone."

The old man's eyes then grew wider.

"I was even afraid to admit it to myself. I did not want to think about it. I did not want to believe it. I did not want to remember it. Every single day since, I have tried to force it from my mind in order to try to live my simple life in peace. I did not want to answer questions. I did not want to face the ridicule. I did not want the attention. I did not want to be hurt. But now…"

The old man smiled at his granddaughter and her husband as he waved his trembling hands over his thin and withered body.

"But now, my humble life is coming to its natural conclusion. And before I leave this world for the next, I now know it's my duty—my obligation—to tell this story. To tell His story. He trusted me to tell it and out of cowardly fear for my own wellbeing, I bit my tongue and kept silent. I did not honor His trust, kindness, and pure love. Out of fear for myself, I betrayed that trust and love. And for all these years, I have been consumed by shame and sorrow. Well, no more. No more. With my time now drawing very close—and out of my own love for you and your beautiful children—I will now tell the story I should have told years ago. A story I should have spread from every village and town to the next until my voice left me. A story that will…change the world."

Benjamin looked at his wife as he narrowed his eyes and ever so slightly shook his head in frustration and annoyance.

While elderly and frail, the old man's senses and mind were still quite sharp. He instantly noticed the negative reaction from Benjamin and then afforded himself a slight smile.

It was precisely this kind of reaction, he said to himself, *which wrongfully frightened me into silence for these seventy long years.*

Leah looked over at her husband and put her hand on his. Like her grandfather sitting before her, and her father when he was alive, Benjamin was but a simple shepherd. More than that, he was a very good man and a loving husband and father. Day after day, week after week, and year after year, he worked endless hours in the worst weather possible to try and provide the barest of essentials for his wife and children. Just like every person and family in the village and the surrounding area, each new dawn presented yet another obstacle to his and their survival. Every day was a fight just to live and because of that, Leah knew that Benjamin sometimes lacked the patience to deal with that which distracted him from overcoming these harsh realities of life.

While uneducated, Benjamin was a wise man beyond his years and believed he knew where this story was going. It was going to have something to do with that *myth*. That fable about the man who walked in this same village and the surrounding towns some four decades before Benjamin and Leah were even born. The man who performed miracles and came from somewhere up in the sky to save humanity.

Benjamin did not have time for myths or for fables. His only concern was to provide for his family while remaining as invisible as possible to the authorities. Roman or otherwise.

He knew Leah loved her grandfather very much. He himself loved the old man. An old man who he knew went through so many terrible things in his own life yet never complained.

Benjamin also knew the end for the old man was not far off. So, because of that and because of his wife's love for him and his for her, he would swallow his frustration and remain silent should the old man start to tell a story regarding the mystery man from over seventy years ago.

Leah looked into her husband's eyes. He smiled back, squeezed her hand and then slightly nodded his head.

Leah returned smile for the man she loved so much and then squeezed his hand even harder in a non-verbal thank you for his understanding.

She then turned back to face her grandfather who was sitting before them with a very bemused look on his face. A look which told her that "non-verbal" or otherwise, he understood all that was going on between her and Benjamin.

Leah rose from the table and walked over to a small container of water. From it, she poured a small amount into a stone cup. She then sat back down at the table and placed the cup of water before her grandfather.

"Tell us your story, grandfather." She smiled. "Tell us your story."

The old man lifted the stone cup with his right hand and took a sip of the refreshing water. With that hand now trembling even more from the effort, he quickly put the cup back on the table, cleared his throat, and began.

CHAPTER TWO

"I was by then, nine years old," said the old man as he looked at Leah and her husband. "As you may remember, by that time, I had been on my own for a number of months. Some soldiers had burned down our village and killed everyone there including my parents and my younger brother. Just before they came, my mother had sent me to the river to get more water for our home. Just as I arrived at the river, I saw the soldiers on horses coming over the horizon. Hundreds of them. I ran in the woods and hid. From over a mile away I heard the screams and then saw the flames. My mother had always taught my brother and myself that if there was ever any trouble to hide in the woods and stay there until we were sure it was over. I wanted to run back. I wanted to help. But my mother made me promise to honor her request…"

The old man paused to take another sip of water. If anything, his hand shook even worse this time.

After her grandfather had put the cup back on the table, Leah leaned over and touched the back of his right hand.

"Grandfather," she said with a deep look of concern in her green eyes. "If the telling of this story is going to upset you, please stop."

"No," answered the old man with a small but genuine smile. "No. I will be alright. The telling of this story just naturally made me think about my mother, my father, and my brother and how much I have missed them all these years. But while I truly do miss them, I know that I will be with them again soon. Very soon."

Benjamin and Leah each stole a quick glance at the other with that remark.

Leah then caressed the back of her grandfather's hand. "Are you sure you want to tell this story?"

The old man's smile grew wider. "Not only am I sure. It is a story I *must* tell. More than anything, I know now that it is my solemn duty to *Him* to tell this story. So, yes…I am sure."

The old man then patted his granddaughter's hand.

"Now…where was I?" he asked of Benjamin and Leah, as well as himself. "Oh, yes. I was hiding in the woods…"

***

"…I hid out in the woods all night," continued the old man. "When the morning came, I could no longer hear the screams and the crying, and the huge red and yellow flames which enveloped the village had turned to clouds of gray and white smoke. I then came out of the woods and walked slowly and very cautiously back to my village. I walked back there *knowing* what I would find. When I came to the smoldering pile of rubble that had been our simple home just the day before, I saw the burned remains of my mother, my father, and my little brother. As soon as I did, I burst into tears over my loss and the shame I felt for not trying to help and ran as fast as I could away from that horrible scene. I just ran, and ran, and ran. It was a scene I have not been able to free from my mind for all of these decades since."

The old man paused again, collected himself, and then went on with a story that was now beginning to transfix Leah and even, it seemed, Benjamin.

"From that moment on, I was alone. Alone. I became nothing more than a street urchin. Less than human to most and even less than animal, really, as all the animals I encountered were at least part of a family or a herd. I was nothing. I was a filthy and hungry little child now alone in the world. Not only did no one want me, but the sight of me either scared people or made them ashamed that they could not help me. Because of that, all pushed me away.

"I knew if I were to survive I had to get myself to a city. For it was there, I would be able to find scraps of food in the trash of the homes or eat from the slop given to the livestock in the stables. After many weeks of living off the land and walking mostly at night to avoid the soldiers and robbers, that survival instinct finally brought me to Jerusalem.

"I do not remember the exact dates now as they have all run together in my head, but just several days after arriving in that walled city, I encountered something quite disturbing. Something obscene in its cruelty. By then, I had been on my own for quite a while and had witnessed much of the barbaric things one man could do to another. But the sight before me truly shocked me. For while I was but a boy of nine years of age, my experiences with the savagery of humans made me old beyond my years. *Very* old…"

Leah took a quick look over to the corner to make sure her son, age three, and her daughter, age five, were still sound asleep.

The old man saw the shift in his granddaughter's eyes and fully understood. He waited until her attention was back on him and it was clear that she was ready for the story to continue.

"…It was only morning but still, there was a very large and very loud crowd up ahead lining the street. Many of the people seemed angry and were yelling obscenities at someone in the middle of the street. From the alley I was in, I saw flashes of white cloth, sweat and blood covered flesh, and a great beam of wood. When I finally made my way through the crowd to stand on the edge of the narrow street, I saw a man of about thirty years of age half carrying and half dragging a large and very heavy wooden cross. Because of the brutality I had already witnessed in life, I knew the purpose of that cross. I knew it all too well. The Romans used them to crucify criminals and those opposed to them. I had seen many crucified men in my travels, but I had never seen a man like the one now before me in this street of Jerusalem. For one thing, pressed down around His sweat drenched, long, dark hair, was some kind of crown. But it was a crown of thorns. *Thorns.* Why He was being forced to wear it, I did not know or understand. But the thorns of the crown were pressed so tightly into His head that blood poured from the wounds and covered his face…"

Even though she felt she had prepared herself for whatever her grandfather might say, Leah was still surprised at how tense she was becoming and at the new emotions starting to well up inside of her.

Sensing this to be the case, Benjamin reached over and took his wife's hand. While he did so to comfort her, he was also stirring with new emotions as his own mind began to race.

"…this man," continued Leah's grandfather. "Was no criminal. I had seen and evaded many in the previous months and I had never seen a face like the one now before me. Never. For even though He was clearly in great pain, even though He was exhausted to the point of collapse, even as some people lining the streets screamed at Him with hateful twisted faces while spitting upon Him, and even as the Roman soldiers walking on either side of Him shoved him from one side of the street to another in some kind of game to see if they could make Him fall, His face…His face…was a face of kindness. A face of tranquility. His face was that of a man totally at peace with Himself.

"After another minute or so, His procession of pain took Him just feet from where I was standing in the crowd. It was at that moment that I noticed His back. I could barely look. He had been whipped and had many long open and bleeding wounds all over His back.

As I stared at that horrible sight, He suddenly stumbled from the tremendous weight of the heavy timber cross and fell to the street. Not only did no one help him, but many in the crowd laughed and cheered at the sight and at His pain while continuing to spit at Him.

"I looked up one side of the street and then the other, and no one was moving to help this poor man. No one. It was at that point that I ran out from the crowd to stand by His side. Other than wanting desperately to help, I had no idea what I was doing. My only thought was to try the best I could with my emaciated nine-year-old body, to lift the weight of the cross off of Him so he could at least stand again.

"As I stepped closer to put my shoulder into the cross to lift it, His head was almost touching the street in exhaustion as blood and sweat poured from it onto the dirt He had collapsed upon. When He noticed someone was next to Him and trying to help, He slowly turned his face up and towards me. His first look seemed to be one of surprise that it was a little boy next to Him. His next look—and all of this took place in but a few seconds—was something I had never ever seen before. He reached up with his trembling arm and touched my hand as He smiled up at me while mouthing the words "thank you" from a body too broken to speak. But it was His eyes. His eyes which spoke most loudly of all. As His hand briefly touched mine, I notice there was a light which poured out of His eyes directly into my own. A real light. I swear. I felt an energy. I truly did. It was an energy of joy, of peace, and most strangely to me, an energy of…forgiveness. He continued to smile up at me and then nodded His head ever so slightly as if confirming something and then…and then…one of the Roman soldiers next to him rushed over toward us and with the hilt of his sword, smashed me in the head. I was knocked to the ground senseless and then felt my feet being grabbed by what looked like another soldier as I was dragged off to the side of the street. That was the last thing I remembered before everything turned black."

The old man then caught his breath as his eyes began to water with the long ago memory.

"Are you alright, grandfather?" Asked Leah.

The old man looked up from the table and smiled at his granddaughter.

"Oh, yes," he said as his voice which seemed to gather strength. "I have actually never been better."

Benjamin looked down and saw that the old man's cup was empty. "Would you like a little more water, grandfather?"

"Yes, please," answered the old man while still smiling. "My throat seems to be getting quite dry as I talk."

Benjamin picked up the small stone cup, walked over to the wooden bucket in a corner of the room, and submerged the cup in the water inside. He then returned to the table and placed the now dripping cup of water back before the old man.

This time, the old man grasped the cup with both of his hands, raised it to his lips and drank until the water was gone. As he was placing it back on the table, it slipped from his weak and bony hands and crashed on the coarse wood of the tabletop, making a noise loud enough to wake the children.

While both children were now stirring on their humble bed of straw, only the young girl spoke.

"Is everything alright, Mama?"

Leah jumped up from the table and walked quickly over to the corner to comfort her children.

"Yes, it is, Hannah," smiled Leah as she slowly stroked her daughter's light brown hair. "We just dropped a cup on the table. Be still now and go back to sleep."

Leah then looked over at her small son whose eyes were fluttering and already beginning to close again.

"You too, Joseph. Back to your sweet dreams."

With his eyes now fully shut, the tiny boy mumbled something and was once again fast asleep.

Hannah giggled and then held out both arms to her mother. Leah smiled down at her beautiful young daughter and leaned down to give her a hug.

"Off to sleep, my precious Hannah," she said. "We will try not to make any more noise."

After sitting next to them for another few minutes, Leah was pleased to see that both of her children were now back to sleep.

She then stood and walked back over to the table. As she sat back down on the bench next to her husband, she lovingly and softly ran the back of her fingertips across the dark beard covering his face.

"I am so very sorry, granddaughter," said the old man as he turned back to face her and Benjamin after looking at their children.

"They are fine, grandfather, and already back to sleep."

The old man nodded but still had a frown displayed on his heavily wrinkled face.

"I am happy to hear that. May I continue?"

Surprisingly to both the old man and Leah, it was Benjamin who answered.

"Please," he said with real and unexpected enthusiasm. "We are very interested in hearing your story and most especially, its outcome."

CHAPTER THREE

"Alright. Yes," began the old man again. "Back to the city of Jerusalem many years before your birth."

The old man then stopped for a second as he seemed to be organizing his thoughts and memories. Thoughts and memories which were now seventy years old.

"Yes," the old man said as his watery and bloodshot eyes seemed not to be looking at Leah and Benjamin anymore, but at something from that faraway time.

"When I came back to my senses—and with a great deal of dried blood now covering a large lump and cut on my forehead where the solider had struck me—the bloody and beaten man with the crown of thorns carrying and dragging that heavy cross was gone. He was gone and so was the angry and screaming crowd.

"The street before me was now empty.

"As I had been for the last number of months, I was once again all alone. And yet now…strangely to me…I was *not*. How could that be? For the first time since I had lost my family, I did not *feel* alone."

Leah could not help but look at her children again with love and deep gratitude that they were not alone in such a cruel world. Just as she could not help but look at her grandfather now with renewed and increased pride because of the good and humble man he had been his whole life.

"I cannot explain it," continued Leah's grandfather. "Nor do I expect you to believe it, but for as long as I could remember up until that moment, I had always been scared. *Very* scared. Scared of the bad people. Scared of starving. And most especially, scared to be all alone in the world. But then, when this bloody and beaten man touched my hand and looked me in the eyes and smiled, all of that fear and loneliness seemed to burn from my body and disappear in that flash of light. A real flash of light which came directly from His eyes. Even though I was now by myself, I was no longer...alone."

Leah next took a subtle sideways glance at her husband at the conclusion of that last sentence from her grandfather and was once again surprised to see that he was becoming more and more engrossed in the story. Gone were his looks of frustration, annoyance, and even disbelief. Replaced now by curiosity and even it seemed to Leah, a bit of wonder as a myth of a man from two generations before was becoming more real with each passing word of the story.

The old man also noticed the change in Benjamin and was relieved to note it.

Ever since Leah and Benjamin had taken him into their home just over five years ago after he lost his wife to illness, the old man had expanded his already good opinion of Benjamin almost on a weekly basis.

First and foremost, because of the kindness and generosity Benjamin had showed him. The old man knew that Benjamin and Leah were having a very difficult time just feeding and taking care of themselves and their children. And yet, when Leah asked Benjamin to take in her grandfather, Benjamin did not hesitate as he was a strong believer in families looking out for families.

The old man did not blame Benjamin one bit for his earlier attitude of frustration, annoyance, or even fear. Over the last number of years, the old man himself had seen a few other village elders attempt to speak about the myth of this man from the cross and watched them pay a price for speaking out. Most of the time, that price was to be ridiculed and ignored. A few of the times however, the price was much more severe as the elders were informed upon to the village leaders or even the Romans.

No. The old man did not blame Benjamin at all for being cautious. All the opposite. He knew this good young man sitting across from him put the welfare of Leah and their children well before his own and the old man owed him nothing but thanks for his always unselfish ways.

"Please don't stop," said Benjamin in a deep by slightly wavering voice. "Please continue with this story."

"Of course," smiled the old man in response. "I will continue. Nothing is more important to me than to tell you two His story. I realize now that this telling…this telling of this story…of His story… is and …was…my destiny. It's what I must do before I…"

The old man's voice trailed off as he saw the faces of Leah and even Benjamin turn sad with the implied message of his last words.

He raised his voice a little in an attempt to distract from that sadness.

"So…" he began again. "Back to the bloody and beaten man carrying the cross. He was gone and the angry crowd was gone, but as my mind began to clear from the blow from the soldier's sword, I remembered something. I remembered the place in the city where they would crucify criminals and those opposed to their rule. I knew if I walked there, I would once again come face to face with the bloody and beaten man who had somehow changed my life forever with one look from His loving, kind, and benevolent eyes."

"Even if I did not know of this place," continued the old man as he looked down intently at the dirt floor as if searching for something there. "This bloody and beaten man still would have been very easy to find. I simply had to follow the still visible trail in the street where the heavy wooden cross carved a narrow ditch in the ground. And even if that had not been there, then I only had to follow the trail of blood He had left in the street as the soldiers and crowd propelled Him toward *His* destiny.

"That trail led to a small hill just outside the walls of the city. As I walked toward it and my mind and eyes cleared yet even more from the soldier's blow to my head, I saw a large group of people. Strangely, at least to me, the crowd now seemed to be made up of mostly women. Even from a distance of a couple hundred yards, it was still very easy—and sickening—to see that three men had already been crucified. The cross of the man in the middle had been elevated about a yard higher than the ones on either side of him. Even though I knew exactly what to expect and what I was walking towards, the second I was close enough to see the face of the figure nailed to the middle cross and recognize it as the bloody and beaten man from the street who touched me so, it still took my breath away in unbearable sadness at the cruelty…"

Suddenly and without warning, as the old man uttered that last word, in the corner of the room, three-year-old Joseph screamed out in his sleep. Leah's olive-skinned face turned white from fear and shock at the intensity of the scream. Before Benjamin or the old man knew it, Leah was by little Joseph's side cradling his head in her arms while caressing his forehead with the fingertips of her right hand.

No one spoke for over a minute as Benjamin and the old man looked first at each other in wonder and then over at Leah and the children.

Hannah had woken with the scream and looked over at her mother cradling and rocking Joseph gently in her arms.

"What's wrong with Joseph, Mama?"

Leah was still staring at Joseph with the deepest of concern and did not seem to hear the question posed by her daughter.

Hannah then reached up and tugged on the sleeve of her mother. "Mama. What's wrong? What's wrong with Joseph?"

Leah snapped out of the fear that gripped her and shifted her eyes to look down at her daughter.

"Oh, nothing, my sweet Hannah," said Leah with a forced smile. "I think Joseph just had a little bit of a bad dream but he is fine now."

Leah then shifted her eyes back to her surprisingly still sleeping son as she tried to convince herself that what she had just told Hannah was, in fact, true.

Leah then knelt next to her children for several more minutes until both were finally back to sleep.

When she stood, there was a new look in her eyes. A combination of concern and confusion.

Leah then walked over and touched her husband on the shoulder while looking directly at her grandfather.

"Grandfather," said Leah with her heart now racing more than normal. "Do you mind if I speak with Benjamin outside for a moment?"

The old man quickly looked over at his once again sleeping great-grandchildren, and then up at his beloved granddaughter.

"Of course not, my child. I think I understand. Please take as much time as you need..."

The old man then paused to offer a knowing smile before continuing. "...I will still be here when you come back in...but... don't take *too* long."

As Benjamin stood from the bench, he and Leah again exchanged another quick look of worry regarding the old man's request.

After they exited through the thick and dirty blue blanket which acted as the only door to their one room home, Leah instantly tried to calm herself by taking slow and deliberate breaths of the cool night air.

When she felt better and after her heartbeat seemed to settle back to normal, she motioned Benjamin to move about fifty feet further away from their home to stand next to a lone palm tree.

CHAPTER FOUR

As the two of them stood there under the cloudless nighttime sky, Benjamin turned his head to look up in wonder at the thousands of stars shining and twinkling above them.

As Benjamin was looking up in awe at the crystal clear magnificence of those stars, Leah was looking straight at him.

After a few more seconds, Benjamin felt the weight of his wife's stare and looked down from the stars to focus on her beautiful face reflected in the faint Heavenly light from above.

"Yes, my wife?" The simple shepherd smiled. "I believe I know what's on your mind."

Leah stepped closer to her husband as she held out her right hand. Once he closed his calloused and weathered hand around hers, she spoke.

"Yes," began Leah as her eyes grew wider. "I am not sure what just happened in there or what made Joseph scream out like that, but something inside of me—something I have never felt before—tells me that it is somehow connected to my grandfather's story."

Benjamin looked up again at the stars in the nighttime sky before looking back down at the woman who had become his life.

"I know," said Benjamin as he paused to move some of his long and thick black hair from the front of his face after a small gust of wind passed by. "I know. I felt the same thing myself, my wife."

"So then we agree," answered Leah. "We will ask my grandfather to stop telling us his story."

Benjamin released his wife's hands and then placed both of his on her shoulders as he looked down at her and smiled.

"Believe it or not, my wife, no. We don't agree."

"But...but," stammered Leah. "What do you mean? From the very beginning of my grandfather's story, your face and expressions made it clear to me that you would rather not hear it."

Not far from them, in the small pen Benjamin had built to house his flock of sheep, a baby lamb softly cried out.

"I guess he's looking for the attention of his mother," laughed Benjamin at the interruption.

"Don't change the subject, my husband," said Leah as a scowl altered the natural beauty of her face.

"But I am not," protested Benjamin. "It is the *same* subject. It really is. That little lamb called out because it needed its mother. As you just said to me, something I have never felt before until the hearing of your grandfather's story, tells me that Joseph was crying out for you as well. But that same unexplained feeling tells me that his scream, while connected to the story, was not a bad thing. Something tells me it was as if an image or a truth was planted in his mind and the sensation startled him in his sleep."

"How can you say such a thing? Where does such a thought even come from?"

"Because...because," responded Benjamin as he took his right hand from his wife's shoulder and placed it on the side of his head. "I believe I felt the same sensation. Just before Joseph cried out, I felt a surge of energy in my own mind. It was an energy I have never felt before."

"But…"

"I know," nodded Benjamin again. "I know. I have always been the skeptic. The doubter. The one who never had the time or the openness to believe in a higher power or to believe in…God. For me, it has always been work, provide for my family and then work some more. That was it."

"Yes," agreed Leah with the beginning of a smile. "I was always the one who wondered about God and Heaven but kept those thoughts to myself. So how can your mind change so suddenly? How can one story or one feeling open your mind now to these unbelievable thoughts?"

"I do not know, my wife. I do not know. I am but the laborer in the family. The beast of burden. You are the thinker," laughed Benjamin.

"Benjamin…"

"Alright," said Benjamin as he held up his hand. "I will be serious. Again, the honest answer is I truly don't know. Like you, I love and respect your grandfather. I always have. He is a very good man who has been through so many terrible things in his life. First with his childhood and then with the loss of your mother and her husband and then his wife. Since the day we took him into our home, I have always respected him for his strength and his morals. But even with that respect and over the last number of years, I have never seen him show so much passion for anything like he is doing tonight. Never. It's as if the very last fiber of his being is telling him he *has* to tell us this story and he has to tell it to us *tonight*."

"I agree with everything you just said, my husband. Everything. But maybe some stories should not be heard after all. Because with this story comes a force we have never encountered before. Of that I am sure."

"Yes," nodded Benjamin as his eyes once again shifted to the star-filled sky. "And maybe your grandfather's story should be heard more than any other *because* of that force we know nothing about. We have both felt this force tonight. Is that not true?"

"Yes, my husband. It is true."

When Benjamin looked back down from the sky, Leah noticed that his eyes now seemed to glow brighter with a passion her methodical and cautious husband rarely exhibited.

"Tonight," said Benjamin with a growing confidence, "seems to be a night for unexplained but very powerful feelings. When we first stepped out of our home a few minutes ago and I looked up at the nighttime sky in wonder, a memory suddenly flashed in my mind. A memory from when I was but a little boy. A memory that has never entered or clouded my mind again until the very second I turned my face to the sky and it was reignited like a torch in the darkness."

For their entire marriage, Leah knew Benjamin to be a man of very few words. He always let his work and his actions speak for him. Since she had known him, she had never heard him speak so deeply or with so much conviction. Because of that, she knew without a doubt, that this unexpected and unusual change in him was happening for a reason she had to respect.

"What is that memory, my husband?" asked Leah.

Benjamin pointed in the direction of Bethlehem—the city of his birth—about fifteen miles away.

"The memory is from over there. In Bethlehem. When I was about seven years of age, my own elderly grandfather told me a story. A story which I had long ago forgotten or pushed from my mind. A story which just flashed anew in my mind when I looked up at the sky."

Leah looked off in the distance toward Bethlehem before looking back at her husband who was now showing that little boy's excitement in the telling of his own story.

"My grandfather told me," continued Benjamin, "that when *he* was a young man, an incredibly bright white light mysteriously appeared up in the nighttime sky. A light he said which lasted for many nights and glowed with the power of hundreds of the little white stars we are now looking at. Hundreds of them. He told me that this powerful light pointed down to Bethlehem and that it was pointing to the place where a 'King of Kings' would be born."

"A King of Kings?" asked Leah softly.

"Yes," answered Benjamin now in a whisper out of real concern the night winds might carry his words to the wrong place or the wrong people. "A *King of Kings*. I had not thought of that strange title or that strange story until now. A story and a title which matches the time of that myth and that fable we have heard a few of our own village elders speak of in both fear and reverence."

Benjamin then stepped closer and pulled his wife into his chest while hugging her.

"So, my wife," he said as his chin rested on the top of her head, "for those reasons and a growing urgency I cannot begin to explain, I, of all people, now think it's critical that we hear the rest of your grandfather's story. And that we hear it now. Tonight."

CHAPTER FIVE

When Leah and Benjamin reentered their sparse one room home, they were greeted with the sight of the old man kneeling next to their children gently rocking back and forth as he whispered something over and over.

When he noticed his granddaughter and Benjamin come back in, the old man stopped and then attempted to get back on his feet but tumbled onto his side into the dirt from the effort.

Benjamin, who was known for being one of the most powerful men in the village, quickly raced over and gently picked the old man up off the floor and placed him back upon one of the benches at the table.

"Are you alright, grandfather?" asked Leah in a low voice as she took her place at the table opposite of her grandfather.

"Yes, my child," smiled the old man. "I am fine. Just an old man failing to get his body to do what it used to do so easily."

"What were you doing next to the children?" asked Benjamin as he sat down next to his wife.

The old man continued to smile as he looked back and forth between his granddaughter and Benjamin.

"I guess…I guess the best and most truthful answer is that I was talking to *Him*. I was asking that He protect your children and allow them to grow into old age in peace."

Leah brought her hand up to cover her mouth as her grandfather's answer reminded her that in the very tough times they lived in, far too many children did not reach adulthood.

"*Him*?" asked Benjamin. "Do you mean the man from your story? Is that who you were talking to? A man who is no longer on this earth?"

"Yes," answered the old man very hesitantly expecting the worst from Benjamin.

Instead of getting the negative reaction anticipated, the old man was surprised and encouraged when Benjamin leaned over the table toward him and spoke.

"That is what I was hoping," nodded the shepherd. "Please finish your story, grandfather. We need to hear it. I…need to hear it."

***

"Yes," answered the old man as he paused in thought. "My window of time to finish the story is quickly closing so I must…"

"Grandfather, please," interrupted Leah. "Please don't speak like that anymore. It's not true and you have many more years to live."

The old man smiled at Leah, but the smile did not reach his eyes. He then looked over at Benjamin who ever so slightly nodded his head in a shared acknowledgement, then looked back at his granddaughter.

"Yes, my beautiful Leah. I will not speak of my own time on earth again. My words are now reserved exclusively for His story and His message."

"*His* message?" Asked Leah.

"Yes," answered the old man as he shook his head as if to clear it of all thoughts but the story. "His message. I will get to that very soon."

Benjamin looked down at the old man's cup which was still half full of water.

"Do you need any more water or some bread, grandfather?"

"No, thank you. I have all that I need. I truly and finally have all that I need."

Leah then took a long hard look at her grandfather and saw for the first time what she was incapable of seeing just moments before. She realized that she had never seen *his* face so at peace. So tranquil. Whatever the process or whatever the mental journey he was taking, she now knew that he was *truly* happy. She now understood that his inner joy came because he felt he was not only helping them and their children, but fulfilling a long-ago obligation which had weighed so heavily upon his mind for all these years.

As Leah came to comprehend her grandfather's true joy and tranquility, her own face of concern and worry began to soften until a growing smile took its place. A smile she knew she was powerless to stop as it was a smile produced by pure enlightenment.

"Continue your wonderful story, grandfather," said Leah as she felt happiness and even hopefulness building up inside of her. "Tell us your story in any manner you like."

The old man let out a deep breath almost in relief at his granddaughter's answer. As if a final obstacle to the telling of this story had been removed.

"Thank you, my granddaughter. I will try to tell the rest of it as quickly as possible."

"Take your time," answered Leah.

The old man smiled quickly before continuing.

"Yes," he said as he rubbed his hands together for added warmth. "Back to my story. Back to His story."

***

"The man on the middle cross was indeed the bloody and beaten man who had touched me so. As I got closer, I became happy to notice that He was still alive. But then…as that nine-year-old little boy very wise beyond my years with regard to the evil on earth, I became very sad and very frightened by the reality that there was but one end for Him on that cross. He would not come down alive.

"The strangest of feelings and emotions then overtook me. I did not want to get too close as the cruelty of the crucifixion and the enormity of His pain was truly overwhelming to me. But…because of how He had touched me so with His energy and His kindness, I knew that from that moment on, I could not leave Him. More than anything I had ever known in my life, I now knew that my place was by His side. Without understanding why, I knew the bloody and beaten man on the cross would never leave me or ever abandon me and therefore, I would not abandon Him in His time of need.

"The compromise I reached with the conflicting emotions swirling about in my mind was to sit on a hillside about fifty yards away. Far enough away not to have His suffering right in front of me, but close enough to be there for Him. The brutal truth for me at that moment was knowing that there was not one person on earth who cared whether I lived or died. Not one. There was not a person on earth who knew my name or even cared about me. Over the last few months, I had gotten used to that reality. There was no one on earth who would care if I starved in the underworld of Jerusalem or if I sat on a hillside and watched an innocent man slowly perish by crucifixion. There was absolutely no one who cared. Because of that, for months, my feeling was, *if no one else cares what I do or where I am, why should I care?* And I truly didn't.

"But now…but now…I suddenly cared where I was. Now I cared about it more than anything I had cared about in my very young life. I was going to sit on that hillside no matter what. Until the very end.

"As I did sit there and watch, I was not aware of the actual time, but I knew morning was about over. Because I was but a little boy at the time, I am not sure if my imagination created more things in my mind than I truly saw. But on two occasions, I saw Him turn

His head and look in my direction. Both times He did so, I waved at Him and smiled. Both times, I *swear,* He nodded His head while trying to smile back. Sadly, in-between those times either some of the people standing around him or some people and soldiers passing by, still screamed up at him in anger. I could not hear clearly but it sounded like some were screaming, 'Save yourself,' and, 'If you are the Son of God, come down from that cross.' One of the Roman soldiers standing guard yelled up at Him, 'If you are the King of the Jews, save yourself.' To me, these people seemed crazy and cruel beyond reason. Why would they scream at this man so? Why would some of the holy-men from Jerusalem also be screaming at Him so? As I heard their screaming at this man on the cross, I began to cry in my sympathy for Him. How could these adults be so cruel to another adult? Especially when He was being executed in the most horrible way possible. And yet…and yet…His face and expressions said He was above all the hate and the anger and truly at peace with Himself. At one point, one of the men being crucified next to Him said something like: 'Jesus, remember me when you enter your Kingdom.' And then the man who touched me so looked over at the man who spoke to Him and with pure love in His face, replied: '*I tell you the truth. Today you will be with me in paradise.*'"

***

The old man then paused in his storytelling as his entire body seemed to shake. He then looked down at the table as if in a trance, and finished the water in his cup. Without saying a word, Leah refilled the cup and brought it back to the table along with a small piece of bread.

Neither she nor Benjamin could find the words to speak.

The old man ignored the bread but absentmindedly took another sip of the water, licked his lips, and then continued.

***

"As I said, of the crowd gathered around Him and the other two men who had been crucified, most seemed to be women. A few of them were crying openly and holding each other. They seemed to know this special man on the cross and seemed to be crying for Him. Just as I was noticing that, something truly frightening started to happen. Something I had never seen before…or since. By then, it was early afternoon and suddenly, without any warning, the entire sky started to go dark. The whole sky. It was as if in the middle of the day, nightfall was coming. Some of the people gathered around the bloody and beaten man on the cross screamed out in fear and ran away. In my own fear of this unexplainable occurrence, I jumped to my feet as my survival instinct took over. I was very scared as the sky was getting blacker by the second. My mind and my body were telling me to run and hide. But as they were telling me to do so, I looked over at the man on the cross. I looked over at the man who had somehow transformed my life in but a few seconds. I looked over at Him through the unexplainable growing darkness and His face of peace and tranquility had not changed one bit. *Not one bit.* Even with the unimagined pain of His crucifixion and now with the day magically turning to night, His expression did not change. I do not know why, but I suddenly felt…I suddenly *knew*…that He was somehow *expecting* all of this. That whatever was happening was greater than anything I could possibly understand or comprehend. Feeling that, and feeling stronger than ever that I would not abandon Him, I sat back down on the hillside. I was still very scared and shaking like a leaf in the wind so I also remember grasping both of my knees and pulling them tight into my chest for comfort. I did the best I could to calm myself from the mysterious and terrifying darkness, but I was not going to run. I was not going to leave Him.

Ever. Towards what turned out to be the end—or so I thought at the time…"

***

Leah and Benjamin looked at each other as both their eyes went a bit wider with true curiosity and…a growing belief. They then both looked back at the old man who now had tears running down his face.

Chapter Six

"…He tried to speak again. The bloody and beaten man was trying to say something. As I realized He was doing so, I began to inch my way down the hillside to be closer to Him so I might clearly hear His words. It was still almost as dark as night so I had to be careful where I was walking. By then, there were not many people left. Just the crying and caring women, the Roman soldiers, and a few others. I quietly and slowly walked up behind them as I tried to remain unseen and unheard. I did not have to worry. All of their attention was only on Him. Suddenly, everything went totally quiet as He continued to try to speak His final words."

***

Leah and Benjamin were now literally perched on the edge of the bench and more focused than they had ever been in their lives as the old man continued.

***

"The bloody and beaten man with the crown of thorns was almost gone. He had been on that cross for hours. I was honestly amazed that

He was still alive. But not only was He alive, He was trying to speak once more. The whipping, the beatings, the weight of the cross, the crucifixion, the broiling sun, and his body's severe loss of blood and water as he continued to bleed and sweat profusely was more than any human could take and yet…He was still alive and moving his lips as if trying to form words. Maybe He had tried or had spoken before I got there, but this was just the second time I noticed it. At first, He had no voice. None. Then He seemed to lick some of the sweat and blood pouring from His face and swallow it as if to bring moisture to his parched throat. Again, whether He did that or it was my imagination, I do not know for sure. What I do know is that He slowly found His voice again. He slowly regained the ability to talk. His voice was nothing but a whisper in the wind, but it was clear He was now talking."

***

Leah leaned across the table and grabbed her grandfather's wrist in excited anticipation. "What did He *say*, grandfather?"

The old man jumped from the contact and for a split second, seemed surprised and confused that any one was with him or even, *where* he was.

As the old man blinked several times and tried to refocus his mind, Benjamin leaned over and whispered into his wife's ear. "Better we not address him again, my wife, until he is done with his story. It is almost as if his mind has gone back in time to that place and if it comes back fully before the story is complete, I fear we may not learn what your grandfather is so desperate to tell us."

Leah looked at her husband for several seconds and then across the table at her grandfather who still seemed to be momentarily confused and then back at her husband as she nodded her head.

"Yes, my husband. I think you are right. We must let him finish his story without interruptions and at his own pace."

***

After another minute or so, the old man was able to regain his focus and return his mind back to the Jerusalem of seventy years earlier. Back to that bloody and beaten man on the cross.

"In the darkness, in His misery, and in His pain, this man wearing that cruel crown of thorns, was speaking His final words. He had regained His voice, but it was nothing more than an uneven and arid whisper. But He did speak this one last time on that cross. After coughing several times and fighting to clear His throat, He *did* speak. Over the course of a number of minutes, and with the darkness increasing, He did speak. At first He looked up toward the dark sky from the cross and said: '*My God, my God. Why have you forsaken me?*'

"With those chilling words, I also looked up into that dark sky in wonder at who He was addressing. Saying those words also seemed to sap Him of His strength. Just to get those words out required all of His physical and mental strength. It was not until a number of minutes later that He spoke again. He simply declared, '*I am thirsty.*' One of the women there then quickly put a small sponge into a jar of some liquid, then attached the sponge to the branch of a tree and lifted the sponge up until it was resting on his bruised and cracked lips. He seemed to try and taste the liquid and then said, '*It is finished.*'

"The woman brought the branch back down and after she did, the bloody and beaten man wearing the crown of thorns looked up to the dark sky one more time and declared in a strained and tired voice, '*Father. Into your hands I commit my spirit.*'

"After that, He took a very large breath, let it out slowly, and then His head fell back down. *It was over*. His tremendous pain and suffering was over. Along with the women present, I fell to my knees and cried. I cried for a man I barely knew, but I also cried for a man whom I strangely seemed to know better than all others. At that moment, I swear, as but a hungry, frail and abandoned little boy, I cried for humanity over the loss of this very special man."

With the old man's mind now fully back in that time, his eyes grew their widest as he went on with his story.

"As I was on my knees crying for this man, one of the two Roman soldiers there walked over to the man on the cross and pierced His side with a spear to confirm His passing. With that barbaric act, I cried even louder and then...and then...something amazing began to happen. I *swear* it did.

"The ground all around us began to shake and move. Rocks were tumbling down from the hillside. I put my hands in the dirt to steady myself as the movement became more intense. It was like being on the back of a running mule. Just as I put on hands in the dirt, the other Roman soldier suddenly cried out, 'Truly, this was the son of God.'

"As I continued to cling to the shaking and moving earth, I tried to make sense of what the Roman soldier had just screamed out in terror. I then began to ask myself: *Is that it? Is that why this special man was put to death in such a horrible way? Because He was the Son of God? Because they feared Him?* As a little boy, most of what was happening was beyond my comprehension. But even at that, I still knew that the man who had just died on the cross was not a normal man. I knew there was something very special about Him. I knew that His goodness, His spirit, and His energy had touched me somehow and because of that, I knew there had to be a greater meaning to all that was happening. Because of all of that, I was not prepared to leave Him alone. More than anything, even *after* His passing, I somehow felt this was not the end."

***

The old man rubbed his face and eyes as he seemed to be fighting exhaustion…and something else. Something only he could see which was approaching just over his mind's horizon.

After another few seconds of pressing the heel of his palms into his eyes and moving them back and forth, he lowered his hands, blinked several times, and then continued.

"After some more time had passed—and I am sorry that I am not sure how much time had passed or what had transpired as the mysterious and unnatural acts of nature had truly scared me and seemed to blur my young mind—I became aware that the body of the bloody and beaten man was now lying on the ground. Someone had taken Him down from that awful cross and seemed to have positioned him with great respect on the uneven soil around the crucifixion site. It was then that I noticed an older man speaking to the Roman soldiers. I had not seen him earlier but I could tell he was a man of great wealth…"

***

The old man then stopped speaking again as he laughed out loud while looking at Leah and Benjamin. Benjamin stared back intently into the old man's eyes as if trying to look through them to witness the vision which was now filling the old man's mind.

Benjamin had never seen nor heard such passion and was becoming desperate to behold what the old man was now seeing from seventy years before.

"At least…" continued the old man as his laugh suddenly stopped as quickly as it had begun and his face turned dark with a painful memory reborn. "…he seemed wealthy to one who ate from the troughs for livestock and drank from muddy puddles when needed."

Leah drew in her breath again and fought the urge to cry as she did not want to once again interrupt her grandfather's telling of a story that was everything to him. *More* than everything she thought as she brought her eyes down to look at the rough callouses on her own hands in order to distract and steady her emotions.

***

"I heard this wealthy man tell the Roman soldiers that his name was *Joseph* and that he had permission to take the body of the bloody and beaten man with the crown of thorns away for burial. After what happened between the unexplainable acts of the sky turning black and the earth shaking all around them, the Roman soldiers looked relieved to hear that someone was going to take the body.

"The soldiers then eagerly nodded their heads as they waved at the wealthy man to take the body immediately. The man who called himself Joseph then looked over at two men standing off to my left and nodded his head. These men were clearly servants and as soon as the wealthy man nodded his head, they pulled a litter over to the body and gently placed the bloody and beaten man upon it.

"When they were about one hundred yards away, I began to follow them. I did not want to be seen, but I had to see and *know* where they were taking Him. After a number of minutes of walking, we arrived at what seemed to be a burial ground. By the time I snuck up to get a good look, the servants were already carrying the body into a private tomb. Again, I was confused. Why would they bother to put this man who had been crucified like a common criminal in a tomb built for a wealthy man? Why?

"As I said earlier, by the time I had reached Jerusalem as that little boy without a family, I had sadly seen many crucified men and all I had seen had been left on the cross to rot in the sun and be picked at by the animals and birds. Why was *this* crucified man being treated so differently and in such a special way?

"Not long after the servants placed the body in the tomb, several official looking men arrived at its entrance. With them came at least twenty Roman soldiers. As soon as I saw the soldiers, I hid behind some large bushes and then got down on my knees to get further out of their sight. Even though I was now well hidden, I could still see the entrance to the tomb. The official looking men began to speak to the man named Joseph while pointing to the big and battle-hardened Roman soldiers. The man named Joseph then nodded his head and one of the officials yelled out something. As soon as he did, the Roman soldiers immediately began to push a massive circular stone in front of the entrance of the tomb to seal it. The huge stone cover was taller than the tallest Roman soldier and had to weigh as much as three hundred men.

"After the tomb was sealed, the officials spoke briefly to the man called Joseph and then all of them—including the Roman soldiers—walked out of the burial ground. I continued to hide in the bushes until they were well down the road and had turned toward the city. Only when they were well out of sight, did I stand up from my hiding place and turn to move toward the tomb. As soon as I did, I saw two Roman soldiers still there and standing guard outside the tomb. As soon as I saw them, I jumped back down behind the bushes before they could see me.

"Why were the Roman soldiers guarding the tomb of this crucified man when the tomb was now sealed by a massive and unmovable stone cover? Why?"

CHAPTER SEVEN

"Roman soldiers or not," continued the old man, "I was never going to leave the man now in the tomb. As I said, every part of my body and mind was telling me my place was now with Him. I had several apples and figs in my little bag I always carried with me and had enough water to last me a day or two. The bushes were big enough and thick enough to shield me from the sun and weather, yet still had enough spaces where I could see the tomb while being completely hidden from view. I know it makes no sense, but I too, was now standing guard over the bloody and beaten man now dead and sealed inside a tomb forever.

"For the next two hours or so, I sat hidden in the bushes just staring at the tomb and the soldiers guarding it. As I did, my eyelids grew heavier and heavier and I lay down on the ground in a small space within the bushes and closed my eyes…"

***

The next morning when I awoke, I started to notice something truly strange happening. Out of nowhere, a great many people from Jerusalem were coming to look at the tomb. Men, women, families, other soldiers and even some of the holy men from the city. Many, many people. Again, why?

Some walked by from a distance and pointed at the tomb while whispering to each other as they kept walking. Others just came and stood closer to the tomb while only staring but not talking. Some looked for but a few minutes before moving on while others stood there for up to an hour. An hour or longer looking at a *sealed* tomb. Why? Why would anyone do such a thing?

As I said, while I was just a boy at the time, I had seen and experienced far too many things a child should never encounter and yet, I had never seen anything like this.

Why would all these people come to look at the final resting place of a man who was now dead and finally at peace?

Later on that day, I noticed a boy only a few years older than me standing off to the side and staring like the others. But what was different about him was that he seemed to be weeping. Was he a relative? Did he know the man in the tomb? Why was he crying as he looked at the tomb?

He had come to the burial grounds with his parents but had slowly walked off to the side as if to get a better look at something or maybe to be alone with his own thoughts. As he stood there with his arms crossed over his chest and deep in thought, I somehow found the courage to come out from inside the bushes and walk down the hill toward this older boy. Even when I was just two feet to his right, he still did not notice me. Such was his complete concentration. When I looked up at him and quietly said, 'Hello,' and broke this intense concentration, he jumped up in the air as if a hundred bats had just flown out of a cave in front of him. As he composed himself and wiped his eyes, I looked back up at his now flushing face and asked, "Why are you here? Do you know the man in the tomb?"

He looked down at me for several seconds before returning his almost unblinking gaze to the tomb.

"No," he whispered. I do not know him."

"Then why are you here? I asked him. Why are all these people coming from town to stare at the tomb of a poor man who has been crucified?"

Without taking his eyes off the tomb, he answered: "To see."

"To see *what?*" I asked the older boy.

"To see," he said as his voice now cracked a little. "To see if He will come out."

***

My jaw dropped with that statement. I did not understand what this boy was talking about. How could I? How could anyone understand such crazy talk?

I then stepped closer to him and lowered my own voice to a whisper.

"What do you mean? To see if *who* will come out?"

Again, without taking his eyes from the tomb, he pointed straight at it and said: "*The man inside.*"

I looked up at his face, then at his finger pointing at the tomb, and then back up at him and said, 'But the man inside the tomb is *dead.* The Romans killed him on the cross. I saw it myself. How can a dead man come out of a tomb?

The older boy then stopped staring at the tomb covered by the massive stone to look down at me. When he did, aside from the tears, I noticed that his eyes looked both frightened and also…and I do not know why I felt this so certain but I did…his eyes looked strangely hopeful.

As he looked down at me, he spoke again in a strained whisper. "He could come out…" he stated, "…if He is the *Son of God.* People all over town are talking about it. The holy men are trying to get everyone to stop, but it is too late. More and more people are talking about it. *Everyone* is talking about it. I begged my parents to bring me here so I could see for myself.'

I once again looked from him, over to the tomb, and then back at him.

"I have never heard such a story. Is that why the Roman soldiers are outside the tomb? To keep people away?"

"No," said the older boy as he now looked around as if he was scared he might be overheard. "I think they are standing guard to make sure He...*stays* in the tomb."

With those words from the older boy, I instantly felt that energy flow through my entire body again. It was the *same* energy I felt when the bloody and beaten man had touched my hand and looked into my eyes.

I felt it at that exact moment. At the *exact second* the older boy said that, I felt the energy surge through my entire body. I don't know *how* and I don't know *why*, but from that moment on, I was certain that the man inside that tomb was truly the *Son of God* and that He would soon be coming out.

***

When darkness came, I made my way back to the bushes to both hide and to sleep. But sleep would not come. Even though I only slept in fits and starts the night before and my mind and body were still exhausted from the frightening and mysterious events which had just taken place, I still could not sleep. Not after what the older boy had just said. I had never been as excited as I was at that moment and I was determined this night *not* to take my eyes off the tomb of the bloody and beaten man.

With the darkness also came new Roman soldiers to relieve the two guarding the tomb. Except, instead of two new soldiers, there were now four. The Romans had doubled the guard to stand watch over a dead man inside a tomb which had been sealed forever. *Why?* With them, these soldiers brought even more torches which they lit and then placed on both sides of the entrance to the tomb.

From my hiding place in the bushes I could see them. In the flickering and yellow light of the torches, I could see their faces and all four soldiers looked scared. Roman soldiers *scared.* They were very quiet and kept looking from side to side. Why? What were they scared of? What were they looking for? *Who…*were they looking for?

***

At sunrise the next morning—and I think by now, this was the third day since the bloody and beaten man had been killed on the cross—several women who had been at the crucifixion, walked up excitedly to the tomb. Amazingly still wide awake, I heard one of these women tell the Roman soldiers that they were there to anoint the body inside.

I shook my head to clear it after she spoke those words. *How could she, or any of them, anoint a body sealed forever?* I wondered.

No sooner did I have that thought that the earth suddenly began to violently shake again. As it did, a blinding *white streak of light* came down from the sky and hit the massive stone covering the tomb. The force of this light somehow caused this unmovable massive stone to be pushed from the entrance.

When my eyes began to refocus and recover from that tremendous flash of light, I saw—and again, I swear this is true—I saw some kind of *being* dressed entirely in white standing atop the massive stone cover next to the now *open* entrance to the tomb. This being then turned toward the women and the soldiers and said something like, *"The man you seek is no longer there."* Then in a booming voice, he declared: *"He is risen. Just as He said He would."*

At that point, the soldiers dropped their swords, spears, and shields and ran from the tomb in terror.

The *being* then told the women to go inside to look for themselves. When they came out of the tomb, they were both crying and laughing with joy.

I still did not understand all that was happening and did not understand at that moment why these women were so joyful and happy. Because as joyful as they were, as scared, sad, and confused was I. First, these latest unnatural acts once again had my heart beating faster than it had ever beaten. The earth shaking again scared me. The white light from the sky terrified me. And the *being in white* coming down from the sky to talk of the man in the tomb had caused me to question my own sanity. And while I was more frightened than ever for sure, I also felt confused and very sad. How could the bloody and beaten man who touched me so have gotten *out* of that tomb without me seeing him? I had not taken my eyes off it all night. How could a dead man rise and how could He have then gotten out when the massive stone cover was still sealing the entrance? As I wondered about that, a huge sensation of loneliness washed over me as I feared that I might never see this man again. I did not comprehend the impossibility of all that was happening around me as no earthly mind could comprehend such events. Instead, the little boy that I still was in so many ways was simply afraid that my new friend was gone and that for some reason, I now needed Him in my life more than ever.

CHAPTER EIGHT

With every word her grandfather spoke and with every breath he took, Leah noticed him getting more and more weak. When she looked at him, she saw only an exhausted old man in desperate need of sleep.

Her husband Benjamin, however, saw much more clearly than his wife at that moment, and knew the old man's story had to be completed without further interruption. No matter how good or how pure, the intention.

Just as Leah was about to interrupt her grandfather again to check on his welfare, she stopped herself, bit her tongue, and went against her maternal and care-giver instincts to allow her grandfather to finish his story.

Benjamin looked at his wife quickly, nodded his head, and then turned back to the old man in eager anticipation of his next words regarding the amazing man from the tomb.

As the exchange between husband and wife took but seconds, Leah's grandfather continued his story oblivious to the unspoken yet critical conversation.

***

The old man began again:

The women who had come to somehow anoint the body of the bloody and beaten man, were now speaking excitedly among themselves. Because of the distance I was from the tomb and because of my fear and shock, I did not hear everything the *being in White* said to these women, but I did hear him say, *"Tell His disciples the news of this day. Tell them now."*

All of a sudden, as one, the women began to walk down a road away from the tomb at a fast rate of speed. Once again, my decision was easy and had been made for me by the mysterious and Heavenly events of that dawn. My place was now with Him, and to get to Him, I would have to follow these women. Where, I did not know, but wherever they were going is where I had to be.

As before, I walked a hundred yards or so behind them trying not to be seen while also taking the higher ground whenever possible so I could have a clear view of them and where they were headed. The women were now walking even faster in their excitement. It was all I could do to keep them in sight as I trailed behind.

After about one mile down the road, they walked past a man moving slowly but deliberately on the right. By then, mostly out of fear of losing sight of these women, I had crept up to about thirty yards away. From that distance, I could not tell much about the man walking alone on the road except that he was walking tall and had an aura of strength about him. As his head and upper body were covered in a white shawl, I could not see much of his face or features.

The women did not even look in his direction as they went by him rapidly on the left. After they were about twenty feet in front of him, the man with his head covered by the white shawl suddenly called out to them.

"My Marys," he said in a deep but somehow kind voice. *"Where are you going in such a hurry? Do you not recognize me this morning?"*

The women turned to look at the man and their faces went white as the blood seemed to drain from their heads and bodies. They turned to look at each other in shock for but a moment and then ran to the man and threw themselves at His feet.

The women began to wail loudly as one them then cried, "Oh, my Jesus. Oh, my Jesus. It is true. You have risen. You have risen."

Before I knew what had happened, I too, had fallen to my knees with the news. Could this be true? Could the man now before me just yards away, be the bloody and beaten man who had touched me on the street in Jerusalem and who I then witnessed being put to death on the cross? Could such a miracle even be possible?

Now on my knees and with my body suddenly shaking all over, I watched as the man with His head covered by the white shawl reached down and placed the palm of His right hand on the top of the head of each woman. As He did, I saw the ugly and open wound in the back of his hand where the Romans had driven one of the spikes to secure Him to the cross. I *saw* it. I saw the still raw and red wound in the center of His hand with my own eyes. Of that, I was certain. And because I did and because I could see it, I knew the man before me was the one they called "The Son of God." And I now truly knew His name to be "Jesus."

The man named Jesus then reached down and gently helped each woman to their feet. In His soft but firm voice He then said to them: *"Do not be afraid. Do not weep. Instead rejoice. Please find my brothers and tell them I will see them back in Galilee. When they are there, I will appear to them."*

At first, the women would not move. They *could not* move. They just stood there in complete shock. They were looking up at the face of Jesus and it seemed to me that they were not even capable of blinking.

The man named Jesus then smiled a smile which would have lit Jerusalem at night as He spoke to them again.

"Please. You must go to my brothers now and tell them what has happened. They must know as soon as possible so they may prepare for my visits and for my message. Please find them at once."

As the women turned to leave to do as instructed, one of them stopped and slowly walked back to Jesus. Without saying a word, she bent forward and gently kissed the terrible wounds on each of His hands, then went to her knees and gently kissed the wounds on each of His feet. She then stood, looked Him in the eye for a second, smiled, and softly touched His face before turning to join the others.

For many seconds afterwards, Jesus stood by the side of the road and watched these women walk away until they finally rounded a bend and were out of sight.

He then slowly turned back. When He did turn back, He was looking in my direction. I was partially hidden by a tree, but as I peeked out to see Him, there was no doubt that He was looking straight at me. And as He looked, a smile suddenly appeared on His face.

After several more seconds, He nodded His head, and then turned and continued walking down the road in the general direction of the village of Emmaus.

It was now *I* who could not move. It was now *I* who could not think. The bloody and beaten man who I has witnessed being put to death on the cross and who had now risen from His tomb and was walking down a road, had just paused to look at…me.

Me. Of that, there was no doubt.

While still frozen in place by the wonder and impossibility of it all, I next heard a soft voice. But it was a voice I heard only in my head. A voice which comfortingly said: *"Come along, my Little Lamb."*

With this man named Jesus now several hundred yards down the road, I finally found the mental and physical strength to force my body into action and to run after Him as fast as my skinny little legs could carry me.

***

After an hour or so of walking, the man called Jesus stopped and looked back in my direction again as He smiled anew. He then turned and walked from the road into a stand of trees. When I caught up with Him, I noticed that He was on His knees in prayer. After a few more minutes, He rose and looked toward me as I stood behind another tree so as not to be directly in His line of sight.

"You must be hungry, Little Lamb. And thirsty."

I remained silent as I tried to shield even more of my body behind the tree. Even though I knew He was speaking to me, I could not *believe* He was speaking to me.

` *"Yes,"* He continued as He took a step in my direction. *It is you I address. It is you I am speaking to, Little Lamb. Again I say, you must hunger and be of thirst."*

Still nervous to be in His presence and in total disbelief that He was speaking to me, I cautiously stepped a few inches out from the tree to better look at Him and was then amazed to hear my own voice answer. "Yes, I am. But I ran out of food and water last night."

"Did you?" He asked as the slight smile reappeared on His face again. *"Maybe you should take another look at your supplies."*

I did not have to look. I knew I ate the last fig the night before as well as drink the last of the water just before I fell asleep.

He continued to look in my direction as He smiled.

"Are you going to look, Little Lamb?"

I shrugged my shoulders and looked down at my worn cloth sack and water skin which I had laid on the ground next to my feet. I then shook my head, as I looked over at Him.

"Why are you not going to look?"

"Because," I answered Him, "I know they are empty. I finished the water and ate my last fig last night. When I just laid them down now at my feet I felt them still empty."

"Is that so?" he said with His smile now growing even wider.

I looked back down at my cloth sack and water skin and to my amazement, both were now almost bursting at the seams. I picked up the sack, opened it and saw that it was filled with perfectly ripe figs and several apples. I next picked up my water skin to discover that it was full.

I next looked over at Him as He was patiently observing me with now amused look upon His face.

"But, how?" I asked Him.

"Faith, Little Lamb. Faith and goodness of heart. They are everything on this mortal world and you have both in abundance. I saw them in you when you tried to help me on the street…I saw them in you when you cried for me when I was on the cross…and I saw them in you when you took up vigil outside my tomb."

Surely my ears and my mind were now playing tricks on me.

"But how could you see me *outside* of your tomb? How is that possible?"

The man called Jesus then moved His hands up and down over His body.

"Look, Little Lamb. Look at me now. Is it not impossible that I can be standing in front of you now? Is it not impossible that the two of us can be talking? But…I am here. We are talking. Do not be in a rush for every answer, Little Lamb, or to solve every mystery. Do not. Rather, be grateful for your blessings. Be humble. And grow your faith. Now…no more talk. Eat your food and drink your water as our journey together will soon continue."

I truly did not understand all He was saying to me, and yet the one thing I knew was that my cloth sack and water skin had been empty seconds before and were now full. Both were full. It was a miracle. A miracle He had made happen.

As for the mystery of it all, I realized He was right. I did not need to know.

I smiled back at Him, nodded my head in thanks and then sat on the ground to eat and drink my fill.

***

Miracle or not, these were very dark and dangerous times—especially for an orphaned nine-year-old boy—and much of a gift such as this needed to be consumed right away as you never knew when and where your next meal was coming from.

As I began to eat some of my miracle feast, Jesus nodded His head once more and went back down on His knees in prayer.

After eating and drinking as much as my little body would take, I suddenly felt very tired and no matter what I did, I could not keep my eyelids from closing. Every time they did close, I fought to keep them open as I did not want to lose sight of Him. I *could* not lose sight of Him. Not ever.

As I struggled to keep my eyes open, I looked in His direction. He was still on His knees with His back now to me.

"Sleep, Little Lamb. Sleep. You will miss nothing. Your destiny is to be by my side these days and observe. Now close your eyes and sleep."

With the last of His words, my eyelids came down again and I fell gently on my side and slept.

When I awoke, I felt completely refreshed and stronger than I had felt in months. At least as strong as before I lost my family, and in truth, stronger than I had ever felt in my young life.

When I turned to look for Him, I noticed He was now walking out of the woods back toward the road. Just as He reached the road,

He turned back to look at me. When I saw Him do that, I quickly picked up my cloth sack and water skin and began to follow Him. As I did, He nodded His head again as if all were proceeding as planned and then turned to walk down the road.

CHAPTER NINE

As the man named Jesus continued down the road with me trailing behind Him and off to the right, He soon came upon two men standing off to the side. Even at my distance of thirty or forty yards, I could tell they were having some kind of debate and even arguing amongst themselves.

Jesus walked up beside them and stood for several seconds listening to their sometimes heated discussion.

With His white shawl still covering His head and much of His face from the sides, He looked at both men and asked:

"What are you talking about in such a spirited manner?"

The taller of the two men looked at Him with an impatient or even annoyed look upon his face.

"We are discussing," said the darkly bearded man to Jesus. "What *everyone* in Jerusalem and the surrounding area is discussing."

"And what might that be?" asked Jesus as He stood to the side of the two men.

The shorter of the two men looked at Jesus in disbelief. "How can you ask such a question? Are you the *only* person in all of Jerusalem and the surrounding area who does not know the glory of what just happened?"

"Please enlighten one so ignorant."

The two men looked at each other for a moment. As they did, the taller one looked at Jesus as if really noticing the man before him for the first time. It was he, who answered the Messiah.

"We are talking about the man everyone in town is talking about. We are talking about Jesus the Nazarene. He was our leader and our prophet and indeed, the prophet All Mighty in word and deed sent down to this horrible world from God above. We are talking about the man who the high priests and officials handed over to the Romans to be crucified. We are talking about the man who was crucified and then entombed. We are talking about the man who on his third day of burial, rose from that tomb to prove Himself. We are saying we know this miracle took place because some women we know went to His tomb and were met by an angel from Heaven who told them that Jesus had risen from the tomb as He said He would and was now gone. We ourselves are just back from that tomb as we had to see for ourselves."

Jesus stepped closer to them but still remained turned to the side.

"I see. I am beginning to become enlightened. You said you knew this man. That in fact, he was your prophet. And yet, you seem slow to believe in your heart what this prophet told you so you had to go to this tomb yourselves for confirmation. Did he not suffer all these hardships and the tremendous pain you mentioned on behalf of you and all those who believe or will come to believe? Did he not suffer his preordained fate for your greater glory? What is there to debate or argue about other than to honor him and honor his message of love, peace and faith?"

With that, Jesus turned around, and suddenly began walking *back* towards Jerusalem. As He did, the taller of the two men on the side of the road took a step in the direction of Jesus.

"Wait, friend," he said with a growing suspicion on his face. "Where are you going in such a hurry? Darkness will soon be upon us and we are about to camp for the night. Won't you please stay and break bread with us?"

As Jesus was now walking in my direction, I saw Him pause and then smile to Himself before turning back to face the two men on the side of the road.

"Thank you for asking. I will be honored to do so," answered the Messiah.

With that answer, the taller of the two men again paused and looked hard at Jesus for a few seconds. After doing so, he and the other man walked off the side of the road into a stand of trees where they began whispering back and forth as they prepared a fire.

Once the fire was going, the shorter of the two men took several small pieces of bread out of a cloth sack. He then motioned for Jesus to come over and sit by the fire.

"Please, stranger," said the man. "Sit with us and enjoy some bread."

Jesus nodded His head and knelt next to the fire. As the pieces of bread lay on a cloth next to the fire, Jesus suddenly reached over and picked one up. As soon as He did, He then said a blessing over the bread and then blessed the two men before Him on the opposite side of the campfire.

As He did, the taller of the two men leaned forward towards Jesus.

"This is not possible," he said in a volume not much more than a whisper. "Your voice. It is different now. It is a voice from before. It is a voice I once knew. I swear it is. Please, stranger. Take the shawl from your head and face so we may better see you."

Jesus then stood, and in the reflected light of the fire, slowly pulled the shawl from His head and face. As He did, both men let out a cry of shock and joy.

"It is you," cried the taller of the two men. "It is you. Everything the women told us then is true. You have risen and you do walk among us."

At that, he and the other man then stood and ran around the fire to kneel next to Jesus. As they did, both men seemed to become overwhelmed by emotion and broke out in tears. As He had done earlier with the women, Jesus reached out His wounded right hand and placed it first upon the head of the taller man and then his companion. Except this time, there was a different reaction. Both men then softly fell to their sides into an instant sleep.

Jesus observed the two men for several more seconds and then said a quick blessing over them. He then rose and began walking back toward the road and back in the direction of Jerusalem.

As He passed the spot where I was hiding, He said, *"Come Little Lamb. You have much yet to see.'"*

I then jumped up from my hiding place and began to follow Him.

With His back now to me as He walked, He turned His head back in my direction and with a laugh said: *"Don't forget your figs and water, Little Lamb."*

I stopped in my tracks realizing I had left both behind in my haste and excitement to follow Him. I quickly ran back, picked them up, and then continued to follow Him at a distance as we headed back toward Jerusalem.

***

While it was now nighttime, the moon was visible and offered sufficient light to highlight the way. But even if it was darker than the darkest cave, I felt that He could always see through the blackness.

After some time had passed, we arrived at the outskirts of the city. As we did, it became clear to me that Jesus knew *exactly* where He was going.

In the darkness, He turned toward the right and began to walk toward a building that seemed little more than a rundown barn. From a distance of one hundred yards or so, I could see the flickering lights of torches through the gaping holes in the walls.

The Messiah then stopped and looked toward the building for several seconds. He then went back down on His knees to pray.

As He did, I tried to move closer and closer to Him without disturbing Him or His prayer. At that young age, I was still frightened by many things in the world. Both known and unknown. One of them being the dark. I felt very safe and secure when I was near Him and kept moving closer until I was but three feet away.

After a number of minutes in silent prayer, He stood and looked once again toward the worn-down building. As He was looking, I suddenly noticed a man walking away from it and down the road toward us. This man's head was down and he seemed to be in deep thought.

Just as he was about to walk straight into the Messiah, Jesus called out softly to the man, *"Simon. What fills your mind, so?"*

As the tall and thin man stopped in shock, I saw his mouth drop open and his eyes go wide in fear and confusion.

"That voice…" he cried out in the dark of the night. "That voice. I know that voice. Is it possible? Is it really true? Can it be you?"

"It is me, Simon. It is me, my Rock."

Like all, the man fell to his knees as he wrapped his arms around the legs of the Messiah. Jesus laid His right hand upon the head of the man.

"Stand, my Rock. Go back inside and tell the others I am here."

The man jumped to his feet, and even in the very pale light of the moon, I could see an enormous smile spread across his face just before he turned and ran back toward the building. After he ran into the building, the Messiah looked down at me.

"Do not be frightened, Little Lamb, at what is about to happen to you."

Before the words even registered in my mind, I felt a strange whoosh of motion within my mind and around my body and then instantly found myself standing in the corner of a barely lit room. My mind and body were now completely locked in place as I tried to comprehend how I could be standing out in the woods one second, and the very next, standing in the corner of a room.

My mind felt heavy with the confusion and I fought not to pass out on the spot. As my little body wobbled back and forth, I became aware of a group of men sitting around two tables. As I focused on them, I noticed the man I had just seen outside who the Messiah called his Rock waving his arms wildly as he addressed this group of men.

Strangely, while I could see the man's lips moving as he clearly seemed to be raising his voice in excitement, I could not hear a word he was saying. Though I was but twenty feet away in a darkened corner of what looked like an upper loft in the old and decrepit building, I could not yet hear a word the man was speaking.

Then, out of a deep shadow at the other side of the room, I saw the Messiah step out into the light. As He did, He spoke. And when He spoke, I heard.

"May peace be with all of you."

With those words, several of the men present screamed out in terror with two of them running toward a ladder which led down to the ground floor.

"Why are you so frightened?" asked the Messiah. *"You are not looking at a ghost. Why do questions and doubt now arise in your hearts? Do not run. Do not hide. Rather, look closely at my hands and my feet and witness the truth before you. Come over and touch me. Touch my wounds. Feel that it is me. A ghost does not have flesh and bones as I truly have."*

Rather than do as the Messiah asked of them, the men began to whisper among themselves while the two near the ladder stepped even closer to it in fear. Now smiling at those before Him, Jesus spoke again.

"Do you have anything here that I might eat?"

One of the men at the table closest to the Messiah nodded and picked up a piece of fish from the table and then leaned over, and with a hand trembling more by the second, handed it to the Messiah. Jesus then took it from the man who quickly shrank back toward the table. As he did, the Messiah smiled at him, said, *"Thank you,"* and then ate the small piece of fish before their very eyes.

"A ghost," said the Messiah after he chewed and swallowed the fish, *"does not eat, nor does he have flesh and bone. Remember the words I spoke to you before, my brothers. Blessed are all of you today and always. I tell you now that it is true. I have died for your sins, I was buried, and I have risen. Everything written and said about me must be fulfilled. From this day forth, you must go and spread my message. As our Father sent me, so I will soon send you."*

One of the men then hugged the man whom I had seen walking outside.

"It is true, Simon. Everything you just told us is true. Our Lord and Savior has come back to us."

With that, all of the men rushed to kneel around the feet of the Messiah. When all were kneeling, one by one, Jesus placed His right hand upon the head of each. And as He did, He said, *"Receive the Holy Spirit and spread the word. Whose sins you forgive are forgiven them, and whose sins you retain are retained."*

When He was finished, He stepped away from the kneeling men and began to walk away.

One of the men suddenly jumped up. "My Lord," he said with tears streaming down his face. "Are you leaving us now forever?"

He turned back to face them as a smile grew on His face and as He spread His arms wide.

"I will never leave you. Remember that. I will always be with you. I will always be with my flock. You will physically see me again before I go to stand with our Father, but I will always be with you. And then...one day...you will always be with me."

Just as the Messiah finished speaking those words, there was another whooshing sensation in my mind and body, and just as suddenly as I had appeared in the loft, I was once again standing in the woods outside.

As my mind cleared and my body once again stopped trembling, I felt the Messiah put His arm around my shoulder and with a warm and loving laugh, say, *"Come, Little Lamb. Clear your head. You have much yet to see...and remember."*

CHAPTER TEN

Leah's grandfather suddenly paused in the telling of his astonishing story to take in several deep breaths. With his eyes now closed, he grabbed the table with both hands in an attempt to steady himself. After several seconds in this position, he opened his eyes, smiled at Leah and Benjamin, and continued:

My next memory is of a morning. I am not even sure if it was the next morning or several days later as time now somehow always seemed both condensed and expanded when I was with Him. No matter, it was very early on this day as I followed the Messiah as He walked in a purposeful manner.

After some time, we came upon a small stone house and next to it, a man I had seen earlier at the horrible crucifixion and then later, I thought, among those group of men in the loft. The man was pulling up some vegetables from a small garden, but stopped and ran over to Jesus immediately upon seeing Him.

"My Lord," said the man as he fell to his knees. "You bless me again so soon with your presence."

Jesus laid His right hand upon the head of this man.

"And John, you have blessed me with your loyalty and your faith and by taking my mother into your loving care."

When Jesus put His hand down, the man stood and addressed Him.

"It is my solemn duty, my Lord. I will keep her with me always and do everything in my power to protect her."

"Yes, John," answered Jesus. *"I know. That is why I chose you."*

The man nodded and then smiled. "Messiah. Your mother only told me last night of your first visit with her. She told me that you said you wanted to appear to her before all others after your resurrection from the tomb to calm her troubled and grieving mind."

"Yes," Jesus said and smiled back. *"It is true. What loving and loved son would not want to first visit with, console, and then rejoice with his mother after such an event made possible by our Father?"*

At that point, a small and older woman stepped out of the stone house. Her hair and head were covered by a white shawl, with her body covered in a light blue dress. As she walked out into the sunshine, the one named John looked first at her, then at Jesus, then nodded his head and walked into the home from where the woman had just come.

Jesus then stepped up to her as He held out both of His hands. She looked down at His hands with the terrible wounds still clearly visible, and her eyes began to water. She then reached out her own hands and held those of the Lord.

"Woman," said Jesus. *"Do not weep. I have come to speak with you one more time before I go. I want you to know that I will soon go to speak with James. When I meet with him, I will ask him to do something for me and for our Father."*

"My son," said the very kind and gentle looking woman as she took her right hand away from His to wipe her eyes. "James is very troubled now. His mind is very troubled now. Ever since your death and the miracle of what happened afterwards, his mind has not been normal. He has not been normal. He cries much of the day and has been all but motionless."

"Do not worry, woman," smiled Jesus. *"I will calm his troubled mind, just as I will renew his life and instill true and everlasting faith within him. James will soon have a mission which will occupy the rest of his mortal time on this earth."*

"I am so very happy to hear that, my son."

Jesus nodded and then led the older woman over to a small bench on the shade protected side of the house and had her sit. Once she was seated and comfortable, Jesus continued.

"Woman. As you know, since my baptism, I have been blessed with special powers from our Father. I remember—and you remember— the first time I used them. They were used through your request. A request which I tell you now, both surprised and troubled me. I never imagined my first use of such a gift would be to turn some stone jars of water into wine for those attending a wedding. At that time, I did not feel like I was ready to use such a gift in such a superficial way."

"Yes, my Son," replied the woman as she looked up at Jesus with a small smile on her still beautiful face. "I remember it as if it were yesterday and I am sorry again, that I made such a request of you."

"No, woman," said the Messiah as He smiled in return. *"Do not be sorry. It was what our Father wanted. All that happened that day was supposed to happen that way. The time to test my powers was then. At that moment and at that very place. Now, before I go back to our Father, I must use those powers again."*

"What is the meaning of your words, my Son? How will you use your powers?"

"During those few years here I spent going from town to town and home to home to spread my message of our Father, I met a number of people who were very sick, crippled, or in constant pain. Many of them children. I am going to find all of those people now and not only remove their suffering but show them I have risen and let them know their faith will be rewarded."

"Oh, my precious Son," said the woman as she stood, "I now know—and want you to know—that every single second with you was a gift. I am so very proud and truly blessed to be your mother."

In the shade of that tiny and humble house, Jesus leaned forward and gently pulled the woman's slight and frail body into His. For over one minute, He said nothing as He softly stroked her hair. Finally, before separating, He lowered His head and kissed her lovingly on her forehead.

"Thank you, woman. It is I who has been blessed by your love. Your place is now here with John. Stay with him always and you will be safe until the end of your days here. Then...you will rejoin me in paradise."

At that moment, the man named John stepped back out of the house. Jesus looked over at him, at the woman before him, and then back at the man named John, before smiling.

He then placed His right hand on the head of the woman before Him and blessed her. He then stepped over to the man in the doorway and did the same to him.

Finally, He looked at them both for several more seconds, turned, and silently walked away.

***

For the next number of days, the Messiah did as He told His mother He would do. He walked from village to village and house to house looking for those He had met before who were suffering. And as He looked, He found them. The blind, the deaf, the deathly ill, those who seemed not to be able to move their limbs or bodies. Old, young, and infants. Men, women, girls, and boys. Each time He found one, He placed His right hand upon their head and blessed them. And each time He did, the suffering which afflicted them was gone.

In addition to those He sought out, He came across others who were suffering greatly and in unbearable pain. People He had not met during the years He preached His message of love and faith. Like those He had known before, He gently placed His right hand upon their heads and blessed them and in the same instant, healed them.

I had seen a number of miracles since the day I stumbled upon this once bloody and beaten man cruelly being forced to drag that heavy and splintered cross through the streets of Jerusalem, but these miracles I now witnessed were something to behold.

To see the faces of human beings enduring the worst that life had to offer, suddenly and miraculously cured by the loving touch of our Lord was something I will never forget. To see young and old faces twisted by unimagined pain or despair transformed into faces of delight and true peace was the greatest and most wonderful event any human being could witness.

During those days He walked those villages in search of the afflicted, I witnessed it more times than I could count, and every time I did, I not only shed tears of happiness for those now healed, but tears of joy for myself that I had somehow been picked to be in the presence of such grace.

A lonely and nothing little beggar street urchin was now bearing witness to the highest and most awe-inspiring power on earth. A power on earth lovingly used by a once bloody and beaten man sent down from Heaven to save us all.

**

No matter where we walked and no matter the time of day or night, I knew that the Messiah always had a plan and a destination in mind. After days of being with Him, I came to realize there was an unspoken schedule and timeline He had to keep.

Because of that, I was not surprised when once again, in the dark of the night, we were walking back toward that old barn-like building not far outside of the city. As before, I could see splashes of yellowish light from flickering torches within the building. A building where Jesus had met the man he called His "Rock," and a number of others.

As the Messiah looked over at the old building, I looked up at Him.

"Are you going back inside?" I asked Him.

With His always ready smile, He turned from the building to look down at me. *"Yes, Little Lamb. We are going back inside."*

"To meet those same men again?"

"Yes," He answered. *"Those same men and one other. A man who was not there the first time. A man, it seems, who has to see me first in my present form to truly believe in me."*

With that, there was that whooshing sensation again within my mind and around my body, and as before, I was suddenly and amazingly standing in a heavily shadowed corner of the loft of that building.

When my eyes and my mind finally refocused from that miracle of travel, I noticed the same group of men as before sitting around the two tables. With them, but sitting silently and off to himself a bit, was a man I had not seen last time. He was smaller than the rest and seemed out of place to me.

Also as before, from the far side of this upper-loft, Jesus stepped quietly out of the shadows.

As He did, it was the man called Simon or His "Rock," who first noticed Him.

"My Lord!" he exclaimed in renewed excitement.

All heads in the room instantly turned to look at the Messiah.

Standing where I was in my corner, it seemed to me that Jesus made eye contact with each, but then…held…His eye contact with the last man He looked at, the smaller man who was sitting off to the side and seemed not quite part of the group.

As Jesus continued to hold His eye contact, the smaller man seemed to visibly shrink from the powerful and penetrating gaze.

As the Messiah looked at the man, He slowly started to walk toward him. As He did, all heads in the room turned at once again. This time, from looking at the Messiah, to looking at the smaller man sitting off to himself at the end of a bench.

Not a word was spoken. Not one.

The steady and unblinking gaze of the Messiah combined with the silence seemed to unnerve the smaller man.

He suddenly jumped up from the bench and then fell back against the wall of the loft.

"But, how?" he yelled as he fought to regain his footing. "The door to this place is locked. How did you get in? How could you be among us? *How* can you be real?"

The man named Simon then spoke up. "Thomas. It is as we told you. As He said He would, our Lord has risen and is with us."

The smaller man shook his head as his eyes darted back and forth looking for an escape.

"I don't believe it. I can't believe it. It's not possible."

As this smaller man spoke, the Messiah continued to walk until He was standing right in front of the man. The smaller man's eyes now went wide with growing recognition as sweat formed on his forehead.

The Messiah slowly shook His head as he finally addressed the smaller man. *"How sad, my Thomas. Even though the others told you the truth, you do not believe. You see me standing now in front of you risen from the tomb and yet you still do not believe."*

In shame, or out of fear, the smaller man then cast his eyes upon the dirt and straw covered floor. The Messiah then stepped even closer and laid His right hand upon the head of the smaller man.

"Look up, Thomas. Look at me."

The smaller man then ever so slowly lifted his head until he was looking into the always loving eyes of the Lord.

"What will it take," continued Jesus, *"to convince you of the truth before you?"*

The Messiah then paused to look at each of the other men in the dimly lit room before returning His attention to the smaller man still cowering before Him.

"Perhaps," said the Messiah. *"Even though you see me before you, it is physical proof you need. If that is so, then you will have it. Touch the wounds in my hands, Thomas. Touch the wounds in my feet. Put your fingers in the hole in my side made by the spear of the Roman soldier."*

The smaller man now seemed incapable of moving.

"Touch them, Thomas. Touch them, Thomas and...believe," said the Messiah in a very soft but commanding voice.

Ever so slowly, with his right hand now visibly shaking, the smaller man reached out and first, touched the wounds of the hands of Jesus. And then the wounds of His feet. And when this was done, the Messiah opened His clothing and revealed the still unclosed and mortal wound in His side.

As He did, every man in the room sucked in their breath in horror as several of them began to instantly cry at the sight of such barbarism. As the other men reacted in sadness and shock, the man named Thomas then did as he was told. He put his fingers into the open wound in the side of the Messiah.

When he was finished, the smaller man then collapsed to his knees in tears.

"My Lord and my God. I am so sorry. It is you. It is you."

Jesus then closed His clothing as He looked down at the man. *"Thomas. You were unbelieving but now you finally believe. Blessed are those who have never seen or need such proof and still believe."*

Jesus then touched the now weeping man one more time upon his head and then stepped back so He might face all of the men in the loft. *"Brothers,"* he said. *"Remember what the women told you.*

Be next where the women said you should gather and I will see you again."

No sooner had He said the words that I was once again standing in the woods not far from the building. When I came to my senses, He was already walking toward the road.

CHAPTER ELEVEN

At that point, the old man momentarily stopped again as he noticed that both of his hands were now trembling more than ever. Not wanting to further worry his granddaughter and her husband, he quickly folded them together atop the table before going on:

Over the course of the coming days as He walked the countryside—with His "Little Lamb" obediently, lovingly, and most gratefully following along behind—Jesus often stopped simply to observe nature and the animal life all around Him.

More than observe it, He seemed to celebrate it and even become child-like in His joy of being in the midst of such things.

Once, when walking between small villages, He turned His head to the right as He spotted a very colorful butterfly gliding from flower to flower in a nearby field.

At the sight, an exclamation of pure delight poured out of Him as He then broke into a run toward the butterfly. Once next to it, He promptly sat down in the field and just waited.

After He did this, something truly extraordinary began to happen. Something which merely added to my faith in Him.

The gliding and fluttering butterfly immediately landed upon His shoulder. As soon as it did, another butterfly flew over from across the field to land on His other shoulder. Then another, and another, and another. Within but a few minutes, His shoulders and the top of His head were covered by butterflies with hundreds more flying about Him.

As He was painted and framed by the vibrant colors of these little creatures, He looked over at me and with child-like laugher now coming out of Him, declared:

"Look, my Little Lamb. Look and behold some of the natural and wondrous beauty our Father has given us on this mortal world to help instill happiness and inner peace. His gifts of beauty and nature are all around us. We merely need to turn our heads from the troubles of life, open our eyes, and see them. See and enjoy the gifts from our Father."

Over these days, He continually followed His own advice. And each time, He did, He seemed to derive greater and greater pleasure, happiness, and peace from the experience.

At one point in our travels, He noticed a small stream and decided then and there that He had to walk into the middle of the cool and flowing water. I had only seen children do such things in the past. Never an adult. But when He did, like the butterflies before them, small fish suddenly began to swim toward Him and then circle about Him as they gently bumped off His legs and feet. First, it was just a handful, but after just a few minutes, hundreds of these small fish were swimming toward Him and then around Him as they all seemed anxious to get as close to Him as possible.

And as they did, His joyful, infectious, and growing child-like laugh flowed out of Him anew as His hands went into the stream to touch and play with these small fish.

And as He reached down for them, He looked over at me again with His smile.

"How blessed we are, Little Lamb. How blessed we are. Once more I say, we all need to appreciate what our Father has given us. It is all around us and everywhere if we but look. Promise me you will always look."

From the bank of this small stream, I looked over at this once bloody and beaten man who I now knew to be the Son of God. A man who had been sent from Heaven to save us all. A man who was now deriving the greatest of joy from the very creatures His Father had put upon this earth.

"I promise," I answered as His continuing laughter flowed like music into my ears.

***

As He walked and stopped to meditate and pray, this scene would be repeated over and over again as sheep, lambs, and beasts of burden would not only seek Him out, but seem to have a powerful need within *them,* to touch and interact with this man from above while they could. And He…with them.

If I had not seen it with my own eyes, I would not have believed it. But see it I did. Time and time again, these simple animals and creatures sought out and interacted with our Lord.

And as they did, a poor and homeless child, somehow bore witness to it all.

More than just the animals and creatures around Him, every single day that He walked the earth during these amazing and miraculous few weeks, the Messiah would stop to admire and interact with something "created by our Father in Heaven."

At certain points, He would touch and marvel at the magnificence of a tree. The next, he would move His hands slowly through tall grass and wheat and rejoice at how it felt running across His fingertips. At other times, He would lie on His back and look up in wonder at the blue sky during the day, or the star-filled sky of nighttime.

Each time He did, He would eventually look in my direction and speak.

"We are so rich in treasure, Little Lamb. So very rich. Look at the real jewels of life and nature our Father has given to us. Look at them sparkle. Look at them shine. Look at them fly in symmetry across the sky or walk handsomely across a field. Listen as they sing from majestic trees and lift our spirits. Listen as the water ripples and the waves come ashore to calm us. Feel the warm and cool breezes as they move our hair and comfort our skin. Marvel at the feast of color that is the flowers of the world our Father has put here. Feel the power of the sun upon your face. Behold and rejoice, Little Lamb. For they are the true treasures of life. Treasures that so many don't see because their eyes are blinded by false treasures and greed. I tell you now my Little Lamb, these are the true treasures of life created to enrich your life. Cherish them and thank our Father above for his infinite generosity, kindness and love."

"I promise I will," I answered in my now own joyful voice.

"I know you will."

He then looked off in the distance before turning back to look at me. *"Speaking of these treasures, Little Lamb, have you ever seen a body of water so large it could fit a thousand villages?"*

I shook my head no.

"Well, then." He smiled. *"You are about to behold another gift from our Father as well as a place that has become very special to me."*

***

Within seconds of His words, I was staring out at a sight I had never seen during my nine short years on earth. As the sun now broke the horizon to welcome in yet another of these blurred days for me, I looked upon a massive body of water which could indeed fit a thousand villages...or more.

After my mind emerged from the fog of this latest miracle of travel, I noticed the Messiah standing on the shore of this great body of water. Standing and smiling. As He looked across the deep blue liquid which stretched miles in every direction, He seemed incredibly happy and at peace.

After another few minutes of taking it all in, He then turned to look at me.

"Have you been here before?" I asked Him when we made eye contact.

"Oh, yes." He nodded as He began to walk toward a small group of trees off in the distance but still along the shoreline. *"Many times. This water and I share much history together. It surely now is a part of me."*

As a warm gust of wind blew across that water and moved His long and flowing hair about, He stopped quickly, closed His eyes and appeared to relish the experience as He had told me I should.

When the gust finally faded, He seemed—at least to me— to almost reluctantly begin to walk again, as if each moment of experiencing these "treasures from our Father" was becoming more and more meaningful to Him.

After a few minutes, I called out to Him from just behind and to His right.

"Are we going to those trees?"

"Yes, we are."

"What are we going to do when we get there?"

He stopped and looked back at me and smiled. *"You seem to have found your tongue, Little Lamb."*

I giggled and nodded my head. It was true. With each passing day and hour, I was feeling more and more comfortable around Him. While all I had seen had proven to me that He was indeed the Messiah, to me, He had also become much more than that. He had become not only my one and only friend in the world, but now...my *only* family.

As if reading my thoughts, the Messiah waited until I caught up to Him and then gave me a hug, and kissed me atop my head.

"As for your question, we are going to wait, my Little Lamb," He answered after he stepped back from me.

I had never felt so safe or as protected as I did at that moment.

"Wait for what?"

Instead of answering right away, He turned His head to look back out toward the deep blue and totally calm water. After another few seconds of looking, He pointed at something several hundred yards away and just coming into view from around the curving shoreline.

"That," He declared as He began walking again toward the stand of trees now not more than one hundred yards from us.

I looked out toward where He had been pointing and after several seconds, I spotted what He had already seen. It was a small fishing boat with several men onboard.

As the small boat came closer and closer to the shore, the Messiah walked faster toward the group of trees on the shoreline.

Once He reached them, He stepped deep into their shade and turned back to watch the men in the boat.

I caught up to Him and was surprised to see a growing smile spreading across His face. As the men in the boat drifted closer to our position within the trees, His smile became even wider.

"Are we hiding from those men?" I now whispered to the Messiah as I looked out toward the men who were now just coming close enough to make out some of their features.

Instead of answering, the Messiah let out a quick but warm laugh as His eyes stayed focused on the boat.

I then turned my head back to stare closer at the men. What about them would make the Messiah react in such a warm way?

To me, He seemed to be reacting in loving pride the way my parents did with me when I would attempt a simple task they asked of me.

I shifted my eyes from the bobbing boat up to His happy face and whispered again, "What are we doing?"

The Messiah then broke His concentration and looked down at me with genuine love as He patted me atop my head.

"What are we doing? Teaching some valuable lessons, Little Lamb. Teaching some valuable lessons."

I shrugged my shoulders remembering what the Messiah had told me earlier. It was not important for me to have every answer immediately or to solve every mystery.

What was most important, was my faith, and most especially, my faith in Him.

Knowing that now to be the ultimate truth, I turned my head back to look at the men in the boat.

As they had drifted even closer, it was now clear to me what they were doing. They were fishing.

Actually, they were *trying* to fish but didn't seem to be having any luck.

I then recognized one of the fishermen. He was the man the Messiah called his "Rock." He appeared frustrated as he spoke to the others while moving his hands about.

It was at that moment that Jesus stepped out from the deep shade of the trees and walked to the water's edge. Once there, He continued outward until the calm blue water was just above His knees.

He then called out to these fishermen in a loud voice. Except... except...the voice was not His own. It was a voice I did not recognize as His. When I looked closer at Him, I also noticed His features and even the color of His hair seemed to have changed.

I did not know why, but the Messiah clearly wanted to fool the men in the boat for the moment.

"Children," He yelled out, *"have you caught anything yet?"*

The men in the boat then looked toward Him and seemed annoyed—or maybe even embarrassed—by the question.

"No," one of them called back across the water. "What is it to you?"

"Maybe," the Messiah continued, *"you should cast your net on the right side of the boat. You might then be rewarded."*

The same man who had just addressed the Messiah from the boat now began to get angry.

"Stranger," he yelled, "we have cast our net on all sides of the boat and caught nothing. Maybe you should continue your walk up the shore and away from us."

"Try," replied the Messiah.

The one called the "Rock" then put his hand on the arm of the angry fisherman and tried to calm him. As he did, he turned and stared deeply at the Messiah for a number of seconds.

He then turned back to face the other men in the boat and instructed them to throw their net into the right side of the water. They hesitated for a moment as several of them began to protest the request from the man called the "Rock," before ultimately giving in and doing as he asked.

Good thing.

No sooner had they thrown the net off the right side of the boat and into the water, then the boat almost capsized to that side from a tremendous weight which suddenly was pulling it down.

"Fish!" screamed one of the men. "Fish. The net is completely full of fish."

"That is not possible!" yelled another as he and the other men quickly scrambled to try and pull the net into the water.

As they did, one of the men touched the "Rock" on the arm and then pointed toward the Messiah on the shore. "Could that be the Lord?"

This man called the "Rock" then stared intently again at the Messiah who was now transforming back to himself.

"Yes!" he screamed out in joy with his own determination as he then dove into the water and began swimming toward the shore.

By the time the man called the "Rock" had reached the shallow water and could stand, Jesus had fully transformed back into Himself.

The man called the "Rock" was so excited to see the Messiah that as soon as he reached Him, he embraced Him.

After the embrace, Jesus looked at the man with a smile.

"Simon. I want to ask you something in private before our brothers come ashore. Does your reaction now mean that you love and have true faith in me?"

The man then nodded his head energetically. "Yes, my Lord. I love you and my faith has never been stronger."

The Messiah then tilted His head to the side and seemed to turn more serious.

"You are now sure of this love and faith you proclaim?"

As water dripped from his hair and face, the smile vanished from the face of the man Jesus also called "Simon."

"Yes, my Lord. I am more certain of that than anything."

"Good," answered Jesus. *"Then tend my lambs."*

The man then seemed momentarily surprised by the request and it was several seconds before he replied to the Messiah.

"Of course," the man named Simon finally said. "Of course. I will do as you ask."

Jesus Himself then paused for several more seconds while looking intently at Simon.

"You will do so, why? Because you have faith in me and love me more than all of these people and earthy things around us?"

The face of the man called Simon instantly looked hurt with the question.

"My Lord. You are all powerful and know all things. I know you do. Why do you ask me these questions? You know that I love you. You know it."

Jesus looked at him for several more seconds before smiling and patting the man called Simon on the back.

"Yes, Simon. I know you do. I truly do. It is for that reason that I now also ask you to Shepherd my flock. Will you do that for me as well? When I am soon called home, will you Shepherd my flock here on earth?"

The man called Simon now smiled back. "You know I will."

Just as fast as the smile appeared on the face of Jesus, it left.

"Be not so quick to answer, my Rock. I tell you now, to do so will involve great risk and the darkness from those who do not believe will eventually fall heavily upon you."

Amazingly to me, the smile stayed on the face of the one called both the "Rock" and "Simon."

"My Lord. No matter the risk, and no matter the risk to *me*, I am your servant here on earth. *Especially* because of that coming darkness, it is my duty as your servant to Shepherd your flock."

The Messiah put his arm around Simon as he guided him back to the shore. After they reached it, He then turned to address this man again.

"After that darkness, Simon, will come eternal light. I promise you that."

"Yes, my Lord," answered Simon as his eyes shifted quickly to the sky above and then back to the Messiah. "My strong and everlasting faith in you tells me that is so."

Jesus nodded at Simon before turning His gaze to look upon the men still left in the boat.

"It seems," said the Messiah, *"that they have finally succeeded in getting all those fish into the vessel. Let us greet them with a fire*

so that we may cook breakfast. After which, I will tell you where you next need to be."

***

Soon after, all seven of these men were sitting around the fire. None spoke. Not one. Instead, all simply stared at the Messiah and waited.

They did not wait long.

Jesus then stood while holding a small piece of fish cooked on the fire as well as a piece of bread. He blessed both and then blessed each man, one at a time.

When finished, He asked the one called the "Rock" to also stand.

"Simon," He said, *"soon, you will receive a sign. A sign to meet me at the mountaintop. When you do, gather our brothers here and those missing, and go there. I will be waiting for you. My physical time here is coming to a close for now. Look for the sign and meet me."*

The men sitting around the fire looked both shocked and excited by the words from the Messiah.

They kept looking from the one called Simon back to Jesus until Simon then answered.

"I will not miss the sign, My Lord. *We* will not miss the sign. We will be there to meet you at the preordained time. I promise."

With those words from Simon, the Messiah smiled, nodded His head, and then turned and started to walk inland.

After a minute of not knowing what to do, I ran out of the shadows of the trees and joined Him in this walk.

I did so because He was my friend…it was my place… and this was my destiny.

CHAPTER TWELVE

Leah's grandfather continued in an ever weakening voice:

As we traveled on, it became very clear to me that the Messiah, though flesh and bone to be sure, was not like any mortal man on earth. Aside from Him being able to appear in locked rooms and condense time and distance, I also realized that He did not need to eat, drink, or rest. And that He only stopped on occasion so the "Little Lamb" trailing along behind Him, could.

Late in the afternoon when we had come to stop in a garden not far from the city and as I was partaking of my never ending figs, dates, and apples from my cloth sack and then washing them down with my never ending water, I looked over at Him as He was once again kneeling under a tree in prayer to "our" Father.

From the very beginning, I felt—and now, knew—that this destiny of mine, was, for some reason beyond my understanding, to be a silent observer to the Miracle of this man. Because of that feeling, I always remained hesitant, and even afraid, to speak with Him as I did not want to interrupt greatness.

As He finished His prayers, I continued to look over at Him. For the last number of days, I had wanted to tell Him something but remained silent.

As He stood, He turned toward me and smiled.

"Yes, Little Lamb? What seems to be on your mind?"

While, as always, I was initially surprised that He seemed to know my thoughts, after a second or two I knew this also to be part of the greater power I had been blessed to witness.

Even though I had grown more comfortable in speaking with Him, the subject now on my mind, made me a little nervous and tongue-tied.

"I…I was…I was just wondering…I was thinking that maybe…I thought that…"

Jesus stepped closer to me and smiled.

"You want to tell me about the older boy you met outside my tomb and the others who came that day."

Like the little boy I was at the time, I looked down at my hands in nervousness as I nodded my head, "yes."

"Tell me," said the Messiah as He sat down next to me.

Still looking down at my hands and fingernails, I tried my best not to be nervous and to answer the Messiah.

"He was crying. For reasons I did not understand then, this older boy was overcome with emotion from simply standing outside your tomb. Others also cried. Hundreds of people walked by to look. Hundreds. I think many of them felt something very special inside. A powerful feeling that they could not understand. A feeling that I could not understand until my time with you."

The Messiah then closed His eyes as if taking His mind back to that day. When His eyes reopened, His smile grew wider once more. *"Yes. I remember them. I remember them all, my Little Lamb. And since I do, will you now do something for me?"*

My head snapped up in excitement. "Yes, Messiah. Anything."

"Go find that boy and any others who are curious about me and hope to confirm that I have risen, and ask them to be at this garden tomorrow morning at dawn."

I could not believe my ears. He was going to make himself visible to people who were not His followers.

But as He told me that news, I suddenly felt a new fear enter my body. The Romans and the soldiers would see Him for sure and arrest Him again and then hurt Him again. I then told Him of my fear as my young eyes then began to fill with tears of worry for the man who was my only friend and family.

He looked over at me and smiled as He slightly shook His head.

"Do not worry, Little Lamb," He said to me. *"Only those who believe in me or who are open to such belief, will be able to see me and hear me in my present form. For those who do not and for those whose hearts, minds and souls are clouded by darkness, I will be invisible and unheard. So again, Little Lamb, do not worry. Instead, go to the young boy you met and have him tell those who believe or who are open to belief, that I will meet with them at dawn in the garden."*

***

As he tried to continue with his miraculous story of seventy years ago, the old man started to cough violently. With each cough, Leah rubbed his back more forcefully while looking over at Benjamin with a pleading look in her eyes.

Leah decided she could no longer remain silent out of love and concern for a man who always put himself last in life.

"Please stop, grandfather. Please. I know you want to keep telling your story—and we want you to continue it—but you can finish it in the morning."

After a few more coughs, thirty seconds of irregular and labored breathing, and then two more small sips of water, the old man looked at his granddaughter with deep pride and admiration.

"Thank you, my granddaughter. My time and life on earth has not been an easy one, but I can honestly say the fleeting mortal joy I have experienced and have been blessed with in life came first from your mother, and secondly and most especially, from you. Your love and caring after I lost my wife and then your mother not only saved me in my hour of need, but enabled me to go on to witness your marriage to a very good man..."

Humbled, Benjamin reached over and touched the back of the old man's hand.

"...as well as the birth of your two beautiful children," he continued. "Because of that and because of my love for all of you, I must complete the story now. Tonight. It is my duty. Besides..."

The old man paused to once again look at Benjamin and smile regarding a truth shared.

"...Who knows what the morning will bring? But come morning, I am sure of one thing. The new dawn will illuminate *the* overriding truth for both of you and hopefully...many others along the way. Now...where was I again? Oh, yes. Standing in a garden with Jesus awaiting the believers in and around Jerusalem to arrive."

The old man then put his head down and as before, began to stare intently at the wood of the table until his eyes seemed to become defocused which in turn, seemed to refocus his mind.

"I had done what the Messiah had asked me to do. After much searching, I found the older boy who had been crying outside of the tomb and told him that if he wished to see the man who had risen from the tomb, that he needed to be at the garden the next day at dawn. I also told the older boy that he should tell his parents and as many 'believers' as possible."

***

When dawn broke the next morning, as He had done during the previous days, Jesus knelt beneath the high branches of a full tree and silently prayed.

As He did, I remained, as I had done the other days, off to the side, hidden deep inside the shadow of another tree. If anything, I was now *more* hesitant to get too close.

Things were happening quickly. Important things. Miraculous and wondrous things. Things well beyond my understanding.

But all things I knew to be part of *His* greater plan.

While the Messiah had told me that I was somehow a small part of that greater plan, the little boy that I was was still confused by the enormity of all that was happening around me.

Ever since I was a smaller child and especially after I became an orphan, anytime I felt confused or even scared, I tended to hide and watch until I better understood the situation.

While my faith in the Messiah was now total, I still found comfort in hiding and staying out of the way.

It was no different now.

As Him telling me to go find the older boy was a part of *His* plan, then I also realized it had to be the plan of His Father above He spoke about with such devotion and love.

Knowing all of that suddenly made me even *more* scared of doing or saying the wrong thing.

Just as those new worries began to flood into my head and increased my fear, the Messiah's voice suddenly entered my head at the same time to stop them.

"Fear not, Little Lamb. Be yourself. Speak your mind. You... are... a part of our Father's plan."

When His voice stopped echoing in my head, I looked over at Him to discover that His back was to me and that He was unmoving and still in prayer.

And yet...He had not only just clearly spoken to me again *without* speaking, but had succeeded in calming me down.

Other than be amazed one more time, I did not know what to do or say.

Just then, I remembered what my mother and father had always taught me about respecting the parents of my friends.

With that wise and loving advice from the parents I lost so tragically now in my mind, I looked up into the sky toward His "Father" in Heaven and simply and gratefully whispered, "Thank you. I am blessed to be in the presence of your Son."

***

As my worries eased and the dawn continued to break over the garden, I looked toward the far end which faced Jerusalem to wait for the people to arrive. After a half-hour, I was still staring and waiting for the very first person. What was wrong? Had the older boy changed his mind and told no one of the news I had relayed? After the events of the last few days, was no one coming? Would no one come to see the miracle know kneeling in solidary prayer just yards from where I stood?

As I began to fidget and pace beneath my tree, I looked over at Jesus. As the light of the morning sun began to find its way through the branches of the trees, His face and body seemed to glow in a brightness all of their own. As His face and body became more and more illuminated, He remained serenely at peace in His prayer.

As I was l looking at the kindest face I had ever known, I suddenly heard a voice. Then another. And another. I turned my head to look for the voices and saw the older boy I had met walking into the garden with his parents. Behind them, I saw more and more people following.

I looked back at Jesus and then back at the people now flowing into the garden. As they made their way down the slight embankment, I excitedly wondered if they would really see this *Son of God?* Would they behold the miracle now before them? Would they really see the man risen from the tomb?

In but a few seconds, I had my answer. The mother of the older boy quickly stopped in her tracks and pointed toward Jesus still kneeling beneath the tree in prayer. As she did, she fell to her own knees and began crying. Behind her, others began to repeat her actions. First a few. Then tens of people fell to their knees in awe of the sight before them.

As they did, more and more people started arriving at the garden. Within fifteen minutes of the older boy and his parents walking in, there must have been a few hundred people from in and around Jerusalem in the garden. Maybe as many as five hundred or more.

And yet, as many people as there were, they were all very orderly and respectful. I do not know if this was out of shock or fear, or a little bit of both. But all of them stayed about ten yards away from Jesus as they formed a half-circle around Him.

As the men, women and even children walked in and then fell to their knees around Him, Jesus remained silently in prayer. Noticing that, the crowd itself grew silent as it waited.

Not more than two minutes later, Jesus stood. As He did, his entire body was now illuminated by the light of the sun and the crowd of people gasped as one in His presence.

Jesus walked several feet toward them and then stopped and looked up toward the sky as He held his arms out and up by His side. As He did, there were audible and loud gasps from the crowd as the terrible wounds on his hands and feet were now clearly visible for all to see.

The murmuring from the crowd quickly stopped as all eyes and all attention was now focused only on the man and miracle before them. When there was not a sound except a bird singing quietly in a branch above Him, Jesus spoke His first words to the crowd:

"My flock. My precious flock. Blessed are all of you today and always. I tell you now that it is true. I have died for your sins, I was buried, and that I have risen. All of you before me this morning now see this truth. You are the new light of the world. As I have said before in my travels, a city on a hill cannot be hidden. Neither do people light a lamp and put it under a bowl. Instead, they put it on its stand, and it gives light to everyone in the house. Your light is this truth you witness this morning. From this moment forward, let this light shine bright before men that they may see your good deeds while praising our Father in Heaven."

Someone in the crowd then found his voice and shouted, "We must punish the Romans and the officials of our city who did this to you!"

Jesus turned His head to seek out the voice in the crowd and when located, slowly shook His head as He smiled a smile of true peace and contentment.

"No, my son. We must not. We must not. You have heard that it was said an 'eye for an eye and a tooth for a tooth.' But I tell you now, do not resist an evil person. If someone strikes you on the right cheek, turn to him the other also. Do not judge, or you too will be judged. For in the same way you judge others, you will be judged, and with the measure you use, it will be measured to you."

Jesus then stepped closer to the crowd while raising His voice even more.

"I ask you, my son. As I have preached in the past, why do you want such a thing? What will truly be accomplished except the creation of more pain and heartache? Why do you look at the speck of sawdust in your brother's eye and pay no attention to the plank in your own eye? How can you say to your brother, 'Let me take the speck out of your eye,' when all the time there is a plank in your own

eye? First, we must take the plank out of our own eye in order to see clearly enough to remove the speck from another's eye."

The man who addressed Jesus now stood in the crowd with a confused look on his face as he said, "How can you be so calm? Are you not the Son of God as the people all over town have been whispering? The very fact that you have indeed risen from the tomb and are standing before us all this morning confirms that to be true. Because you are the Son of God, you must surely have the power to punish those who sinned against you."

"No, my son," said Jesus as the smile left His face. *"They have only sinned against themselves. They have only hurt themselves. Again, please do not judge lest you be judged. Today, as we greet this Heavenly day, I tell you of the greatest of all commandments. The first and greatest being 'Love the Lord your God with all of your heart and with all of your soul and with all of your mind.' The second being 'Love your neighbor as yourself.' In other words, 'Do to others what you would have them do to you.' Love your enemies and pray for those who persecute you so you may be with our Father in Heaven."*

A woman then stood up next to the man addressing Jesus and spoke up as newly formed tears rolled down her face. "But my Lord," she began while pointing at Him, "look at your hands. Look at your feet. Look at the horrible things they did to you."

Instead of looking down at His hands and feet, Jesus stepped even closer to the crowd.

"No. You look at them. All of you look at them. Look at them. Then look back into my eyes and see the truth. See the truth and see the light. I know what they did but they truly knew not what they were doing. I have forgiven them. For if you forgive men when they sin against you, our Heavenly Father will also forgive you. But if you do not forgive men their sins, our Father in Heaven will not forgive your sins."

As Jesus continued to address the more and more adoring crowd before Him, I noticed two men enter the garden as they tried to also remain out of sight. It was clear they were not trying to join the crowd, but rather, observe it. I then moved up the tree line until I was behind them and yet still only a few yards away. From where I now stood, I heard these two men speak. Both appeared to be officials from the city.

"Look at all of these people," one of them began. "It is true what my servant told me last night. These people have come to see the 'Son of God' risen from the tomb."

The other official then looked at the first as an evil smile spread across his face. "Yes. These simple-minded fools are here to see the man from the tomb. If that man we crucified still truly walks the earth—which I doubt—then we will be ready for him when he comes. Go back now and order the Roman soldiers here immediately. If and when this miracle man enters the garden, we will not only capture him, but finish the job we started. The man who has risen will rise no more."

I could not believe what I was seeing and hearing. The Lord Jesus was standing down at the bottom of the embankment in plain sight of these men but they could not see Him. As I looked at Jesus, He continued to speak to the crowd before Him. And yet...*as He had predicted*...these non-believing city officials in front of me could neither see nor hear Him. He was invisible to them. It was another miracle on top of the many I had witnessed just in these few short weeks.

As the one official went scurrying off to get the Roman soldiers, I made my way back down the hill to stand once again, in the shadow of my tree. Shifting from one foot to the other in my growing nervousness, I listened as Jesus continued to address the crowd gathered before Him.

"Do not store up for yourselves treasure on this earth, where moth and rust destroy, and where thieves break in and steal. But store up for yourselves treasures in Heaven. Worrying about earthly possessions and wealth is a waste of time. It is easier for a camel to go through the eye of a needle than for a rich man to enter the Kingdom of God. For what good will it be for a man if he gains the world yet forfeits his soul? Much better not to worry about these things. Who of you, by worrying, can add a single hour to his life? Store up, instead, on prayer. But when you pray, do not pray like those who need to be seen by many to prove they are worthy. No. When you do pray, go into your room, close the door and pray to our Father, who is unseen but all knowing. Then your Father, who sees what is done in secret, will reward you."

As Jesus spoke, I kept looking up the embankment and toward the entrance to this garden. For it was from there the Roman soldiers would soon appear with their weapons and with blood in their eyes. I was desperate to step out of the shadow and warn Jesus of the impending danger and yet, something kept telling me to hold my place and just wait. That it would all somehow be fine.

And for the moment, it was more than fine. It was *perfect*. I had never seen hundreds of people so silent as they hung on every word that Jesus spoke. They truly would have listened all day, but He seemed to be coming to end of His sermon.

"You now see the truth you sought standing before you. Because you do and because you are here, I tell you that everyone who leaves houses or brothers or sisters or father or mother or fields for my sake will receive a hundred times as much and will inherit eternal life. While on earth, you must look out for one another. You must. But be unselfish and truly loving during your mortal time. For I tell you, blessed are the meek, for they will inherit this earth. Blessed are the peacemakers, for they will be called Sons of God. Blessed are the pure in heart, for they will see God. Blessed are the poor, for theirs

is the Kingdom of Heaven. Blessed are those who hunger and thirst for they will be...filled."

With those last words, He turned His head slightly, made eye contact with me, and...smiled.

After He did, Jesus then stopped His sermon momentarily to walk deep into the center of the crowd. When He stopped, He looked up toward the entrance of the garden and then back at the wide-eyed and excited faces of the people surrounding Him.

"There is trouble coming. You must all leave. But hear this now before you do. As you have all taken a risk to come here this morning to see that I am risen, I tell you now, whoever acknowledges me before men, I will also acknowledge them before my Father in Heaven. But whoever disowns me before men, I will disown them before my Father in Heaven. Those now on the way to this place will never acknowledge me. They will never believe. To believe in me involves great risk. Blessed are you when people insult you, persecute you and falsely say all kinds of evil against you because of me. But when they do, rejoice and be glad, for great is your reward in Heaven. Now go my children. Go. I will see you all later..."

He then paused one last time as He smiled and seemed to look deeply into the eyes of every single person gathered around Him. *"...I promise."*

Such was the power and the presence *of Jesus and* His words that the crowd turned instantly as one and began to walk back out of the garden. As they did, not a single word was spoken amongst them.

Several minutes after they left, the other city official rushed back into the garden followed by at least thirty Roman soldiers. As they did and out of habit, I hid deep inside some very thick bushes next to the trees.

By this time, the official who had waited in the garden, had made his way down to the bottom of the embankment and was standing no more than ten feet away from Jesus once again kneeling in prayer, yet could not see Him. *He could not see Him.* He was ten feet away yet could not see the Messiah. Within seconds, the other official and the Roman soldiers joined him at the bottom of the embankment.

"What happened?" screamed the official who just came back with the Roman soldiers. "I just saw the crowd on the road heading back to the city. Not one of them was speaking or even looked up. Did the miracle man they were waiting for ever show up?"

"No," said the other official in clear disappointment and anger. "He never appeared. I was here the whole time and never took my eyes off this area. Strangely, the crowd just knelt on the ground in silence the whole time. One or two of them stood, but I heard nothing. The man they came to see never showed up."

The other official's face then turned red with rage. "I have already bribed the soldiers who guarded the tomb into silence," he said. "We must do the same with any others who know of this story. We must kill this myth before it can take root among the people. The fable about the man who rose from the tomb must not be allowed to spread. It must not. Let us go back to Jerusalem now to make sure it does not."

As the officials walked rapidly and angrily out of the garden, followed by the Roman soldiers, I noticed one soldier lingering behind as the rest marched out. By his markings, he was clearly an officer.

After the officials and other soldiers were gone, this lone soldier then slowly walked back down the embankment to the area where Jesus was still kneeling in prayer. Even though I knew Jesus was invisible to this soldier, it still seemed to me that the soldier was staring *directly* at our Savior.

Upon standing up from His prayer, Jesus then looked straight into the eyes of the very large and imposing soldier.

"Good morning, my son. Thank you for walking down to greet me."

The Roman soldier looked back over his shoulder to make sure the garden was still empty then dropped to his knees in front of Jesus.

"I saw you," said the soldier as he looked down at the wounded feet of Jesus. "When the others could not see you, I could. I could *see* you. I could *see* you. Why?"

As with the others before, Jesus put his right hand atop the head of the Roman soldier and held it there for several seconds.

"Stand, my son," said the Messiah to the soldier.

The soldier stood but could not bring himself to look at Jesus.

"Look at me, my son."

The Roman officer slowly lifted his head and looked into the eyes of the Lord.

Jesus then placed His right hand on the left shoulder of the soldier.

"You saw me and see me and now hear me because…you believe. Because…you have goodness within you. The others do not. They have darkness within them and will be lost forever if they do not fight it off."

"It is true, then," said the Roman soldier as tears now filled his eyes. "You have risen from the tomb and are the Son of God."

"Yes. It is true. As I said, I died for your sins. I was buried. And I have risen. I ask you now to sin no more. I ask you now to lay down your sword and shield and never inflict pain on another human being. I ask you now to realize there is but one Kingdom and to go out into the world and do good as you spread the word of me and my message. Will you do that for me, my son?"

The soldier immediately fell back to the feet of Jesus.

"Yes, I will, my Lord," he cried. "You have my word. For the rest of my life, I will go in peace and tell as many people as possible of the miracle I witnessed today."

Jesus then once again laid his hand upon the head of the Roman soldier.

"Bless you, my son. Bless you. Now go in peace."

After the soldier slowly walked out of the garden, Jesus turned to look back toward me still hiding in the bushes and laughed at the sight.

"There is no need to hide. As I told you, when you are with me, you will remain invisible to others. Now, come, my Little Lamb. Follow me and continue to observe. My time here is now running short but I have powerful words yet to speak."

CHAPTER THIRTEEN

Leah's grandfather paused yet again in the telling of his extraordinary story as his breathing became more and more labored and forced.

As he did, Leah turned to look at her husband with pleading eyes.

Benjamin felt her same fears and concerns but now knew beyond a shadow of a doubt that it truly was the old man's destiny to tell his story now and that he was using all of his remaining physical and mental strength to do so.

Before Benjamin could respond in any way to his wife, the old man began speaking again:

As we were walking and not long after He had addressed that huge crowd, He looked at me with an expression I had not seen before.

It was both somber and—at least it seemed to me at the time—sad.

"We are now near where my brother is staying. He is greatly troubled and disturbed. I must go to him. I must speak with him before I move on." With that, He turned and began to walk toward the town.

After not many minutes, we were in front of the open doorway to a small home. Jesus stood in front of the open door and softly called out.

"James. It is me. Your brother."

As always, my place was off to the side and out of the way.

Out of the way, but still close enough to hear and to see.

And from where I stood, I could tell there was no answer from within the little home nor any movement. None.

The Messiah spoke again. Only this time, in a firmer voice.

"Brother. Do not hide. Do not be ashamed. Do not avoid me. I love you and always will. Come out and greet the truth which was foretold."

After another minute of silence, a man slowly shuffled to the door. He was about the same height as the Messiah and had thick dark hair and a long dark beard. As he hesitantly crossed the threshold of the door to barely stand outside, his head remained bowed as he stared at the dirt.

The man Jesus had addressed did not seem to understand what was being said to him. Even though I was a number of feet away, I could tell that he was disoriented and maybe even frightened.

After several more seconds, the man ever so slowly lifted his head. When he did, I could see that his eyes were closed. When he finally did open them, he was staring at the face of the Messiah not three feet from his own.

As he looked, his eyes registered the shock he was now feeling.

Seconds after they did, this man, like all who witnessed this miracle before them, fell to the ground crying as he hugged the legs of the Messiah. As he cried uncontrollably, Jesus reached down and gently pulled this man named James to his feet.

"James," said the Messiah as He looked at the man whose head was once again bowed. *"It is so very good to see you, my Brother. I tell you now I must go in but a few moments but I felt it important to see you and tell you that...I love you."*

Upon hearing that, the man named James collapsed back to the ground and brought his head down to his knees while crying out loud.

"Why? Why do you love me? Why? I am not worthy of your love. I rejected you. I tried to turn our mother and the family against you. I questioned your sanity. I told others to question it. I am so very sorry and ashamed of my actions and disbelief and I tell you now, I am not worthy of your love or your attention. I am not worthy and I beg your forgiveness."

Jesus then knelt on the ground next to His brother and pulled the crying man into His chest.

"James. James. All was forgiven long ago. You are worthy because your heart is now open. You are worthy because you now believe. You are worthy because you are a good and decent man. You are worthy because...you are my brother."

The man named James slowly stopped crying and began to compose himself.

"Th...thank you for your forgiveness, brother, and thank you for...for your love. I feel it now. I do. I feel the energy flowing through me. I feel your energy flowing through me."

"James. I must go. My time here is limited. But before I leave, I need to ask you to do something for me. Something very important. It must be done. It must. Will you help me?"

The man named James then smiled as his eyes seemed to beam with pride at the question.

"I will do anything for you My Brother...My...Lord. Anything. I am now and will always remain, your humble servant."

Jesus then stood and James stood with Him.

"Bless you, brother. When the time comes," continued Jesus, *"what I am saying to you now will make sense. When the time comes, you must build upon the foundation Peter starts here in Jerusalem. You must build upon that foundation. Others will run from the responsibility. Out of fear and because they lack true faith, they will run. You must not. You must take a leadership role and then spread my message as far and wide as possible. You must increase the flock and that flock must know that there is a true way out of the darkness. They must know that evil can and will be defeated and that goodness,*

light, and salvation will be their reward for eternity if they honor my message. James, my beloved brother, if you build upon what Peter starts with my message of peace, love, and salvation, you will honor me and stand with me forever in Heaven."

I then saw the man called James reach out and grasp the hands of Jesus. As he did, his eyes—like all others—went wide in shock at the sight of the fresh and vivid wounds in the hands of his brother. When he looked back up to his brother's face, the eyes of Jesus once again seemed to glow with a light of pure love.

As He did with His mother, Jesus then pulled His brother James into His arms and hugged him for many seconds and stroked his hair as He calmed him. When the Messiah stepped back, the man named James began once again to weep.

"Do not cry in sadness, my brother, but in joy. Through the power of our Father, I have risen and with that miracle comes a new beginning for humanity. Spread the word, my brother. Spread the word. People must know of this miracle just as they must know that true faith will guide them to a better word. Spread the word my brother no matter the obstacles, and you will stand with me one day in Paradise."

They embraced one more time and then the Messiah turned and began walking away from the town.

***

I awoke just after dawn from a deep sleep to see the Messiah standing above me and once again smiling a smile bright enough to light the night.

"Come, my Little Lamb. The time has now come for us to set forth on our last earthly journey together."

I jumped to my feet with the sound of His words. As their meaning sank into my still clouded mind, fear and loneliness once again gripped me.

As I rubbed my eyes to clear them while bending down to pick up my sack of food and my water-skin, Jesus was already walking away.

As He walked, He turned to look back at me.

"Do not fear, my Little Lamb. Do not cry. I will always be with you. Though this is our last physical journey together, I promise, as long as you have faith in me and in our Father, I will never leave you, so fret not."

As my tears had instantly appeared after He spoke His first sentence to me, my task was now to wipe them away as I walked behind Him. As His words of love and comfort settled in my now always amazed mind, I began to feel better and relax.

"Where are we going now, Messiah?"

While still walking, He pointed with His right hand to a nearby mountaintop east of the city.

"To the top, Little Lamb. We are going to the very top."

***

As we walked up and up and up toward the mountaintop, my small and weak legs began to tremble from the effort and the steep angle of the trail before me.

I stopped to catch my breath while also laying my cloth sack and water-skin on the ground next to me to further ease my shoulder and legs. After I did, and while taking in great gulps of air, I looked first up at the mountaintop and then down from where we had come.

Even though we were only halfway up the mountain, the view of the city and the surrounding area was like none I had ever seen before. It was beyond magnificent and I knew this very view, was but another one of the treasures the Messiah mentioned which should be both admired and appreciated.

As I tried to take it all in, my breathing was still heavy from the climb.

I then became aware that the Messiah Himself had stopped and was looking back down the trail at me.

"You are tired, Little Lamb. The climb is too much for you."

I smiled up at Him as pure love and joy filled my heart. "No, my Lord," I answered as my breathing was still faster than normal. "I am fine and ready to continue on."

Just as I uttered those words, there was another tremendous whooshing sensation in my mind and around my body and before I knew what was happening, we were standing atop the mountain.

***

Now, I had lost my breath for an entirely different reason. For even though it had happened to me before, my young mind would simply never comprehend the enormity of the miracle which had just transpired.

One second, I was standing halfway up the mountain and out of breath. The very next, I was standing *atop* the mountain and even more out of breath. But not from a labored walk. But rather, out of earthy amazement at a Heavenly act.

When my mind fully cleared, I saw the Messiah look at me and smile. But the smile seemed less than His normal to me. As if He and His mind were preoccupied with other and greater thoughts.

He then looked at the ground where I was standing, looked back up to my eyes and then nodded His head once toward me. Without saying a word, I knew He wanted me to stay where I was. After these last blessed weeks of following along behind Him on His miraculous journey, I had become familiar with His body language. And even if

I had not, the unequalled power of His mind and being, would always communicate any message He wanted.

As I stood there, He walked a number of yards away before coming to a stop. Once at the spot He chose, His head moved ever so slowly back and forth as He looked down upon the city and the countryside for several minutes.

Then, as He had done multiple times a day, and now under a mostly cloud-free blue sky and beneath the warming and welcome rays of the sun, He went down on His knees in prayer.

He then stayed in prayer until we heard the voices.

I turned my head to find the source of the voices and coming up the trail, I saw a group of men being led by the man called the "Rock." All men I had seen before with the Messiah, and all, I had come to learn, were His most loyal followers and disciples.

Jesus stood and turned to face these men.

Now themselves out of breath and even sweating in the crisp and cool air of the mountaintop, they stopped a number of yards away to compose themselves.

As they did, the Lord looked toward me and smiled and then back at the men before Him.

Once ready, all silently walked up to Him and knelt before Him as they bowed their heads. The Messiah then stood in front of each man and placed His right hand upon their heads. When He stood back, He said: *"It is time."*

***

After saying that, the Messiah then turned His head slightly and looked right at me. As before, I realized that even though I was truly flesh and bone, only He could see me at this moment. Only He could hear me. And only *He* knew why.

It was, as He had wanted it to be from the very beginning.

Just six weeks before, I was nothing more than a poor and homeless little beggar boy who happened to stumble upon an act and procession so obscene in its cruelty, that it was all but impossible not to lose faith in all of humanity.

And then...and then...I met Him.

And through Him...I was saved.

Day after day, week after week, I bore witness to the miracles this Son of God made possible. From the very instant that once bloody and beaten man wearing His crown of thorns first touched me on that street in Jerusalem, true faith was born within me.

True and everlasting faith.

Every day since, my faith in Him and my love for Him grew in such ways I never thought possible. But now...but now...this man I loved so...this man who had become my very special and *only* friend on earth was...leaving.

For the little boy that I still was, that knowledge was quickly becoming too much to bear. While He had told me not to be sad, the reality of the moment was overwhelming. I surely would be lost without my best friend on earth.

As my eyes welled-up once again and as my legs began to shake with the immense sadness of that thought, the Messiah spoke directly to me.

But as He did, He did so as He had done before. For even though He was now speaking to me, His mouth never opened and His lips never moved. And yet, even though that was true, His deep and loving voice still spoke loudly within my mind.

"As I have said, do not cry, my Little Lamb. Stay strong and never lose faith. There are challenges yet to come in life. Challenges you will have to overcome. Do the best you can while you are in your mortal form in this mortal and troubled world. Be the best person you can possibly be while being kind and loving to those around you. Especially to those most in need. Never let the growing evil on

this world kill the goodness in your heart and soul. Do not fear the darkness around you. Your goodness is but a small light. But when combined with the goodness of the millions of small lights around this earth, its power will illuminate the path of escape from that darkness and evil and deliver you to eternal salvation."

"Will I see you again?" I haltingly asked Him as I used my sleeve to wipe my nose and eyes as the tears continued to spill down my face.

"Yes. Yes you will, my Little Lamb. You have touched me with your love, your kindness and your unselfishness. Many years from now when you depart this imperfect world, you will see me again."

"Where?" I asked Him, as I felt a surge of energy flowing from His eyes into my little body.

"In Paradise," He said as he smiled at me. *"After all this time with me, you now know that. You will stand beside me in Heaven for eternity. So be good, my Little Lamb. Be good and never ever lose faith. And remember...when the time is right...tell my story. Tell our story. Tell the people what you saw during our weeks together on earth. Tell them of me and tell them of my message of love and peace. And when you do, tell them never to lose faith and never lose faith in me. If you do these things, you and all who believe in me, will see me again in but the blink of an eye. Do this for me, my Little Lamb."*

He then turned His head from me to look at the men kneeling before Him atop the mountain. Men who could not see me and had not heard our conversation. And when He did speak to them, His lips now moved and I heard His words once again through my ears.

"Brothers. I say to you now, as I go back to our Father in Heaven, do not leave this city. Stay until you receive the sign. As John baptized me with water, our Father will soon baptize you with the Holy Spirit."

A man in the middle of the group then spoke up.

"My Lord. Does this mean the Kingdom will now be restored here?"

The Messiah smiled down at him.

"It is not for you to ask such a question nor to question the will or the timing of our Father. Simply know that all powers in Heaven and on earth have been given to me. Knowing that and upon receiving the sign from our Father, go into the world and proclaim my gospel to all and create disciples wherever you go. Baptize them all in the name of the Father, the Son, and the Holy Spirit and teach them all as I have taught you. Do these things and behold, you will stand with me forever."

As soon as He finished speaking those words, the most miraculous thing I had ever witnessed then happened.

With His arms now outstretched by His side, His body ever so slowly began to rise from the ground. As He had risen from that tomb, He was now *physically* rising into the sky before our very eyes.

As He rose in the morning sun, the wounds to His hands and feet were clearly visible to all. Vivid and telling reminders of the pain and sacrifice He had endured and made for us all.

With each passing second, His acceleration into the sky increased. Soon, now hundreds of feet above the earth, the miracle of this journey was obscured by a small white cloud.

The whitest cloud I had ever seen.

As myself and His disciples thirty yards from me stared now straight up while straining our eyes to see Him again, the last miracle of that day happened.

From the very middle of that unnaturally white cloud appeared the *being in white* I had witnessed at the tomb of Jesus on the morning of His resurrection.

The being in white then came straight down from the cloud and suspended himself no more than twenty feet in the air above the heads of the disciples.

"Why," asked the being in white in a booming voice. *"Are you still standing here looking into the sky? Our Jesus who has now gone up into Heaven will return in the same manner at the chosen time. Go now. Honor Him and His sacrifice and proclaim His gospel to the world."*

***

After barely getting out those miraculous and awe-inspiring words from the angel above, Leah's rapidly weakening grandfather came to the end of the story he felt and *knew* it was his destiny to tell.

CHAPTER FOURTEEN

At the conclusion of the old man's story, Leah was in tears. She looked toward her husband and was not surprised to see him turn his head away as he tried and failed to hide the tears in his own eyes.

She then looked back over at her beloved grandfather.

At that instant, he reached across the table and forcefully grabbed her hand.

"It is time my dear Leah. It is now *my* time. I am being called home now. I am being called home to *Him*. I can feel it. I can feel that same surge of energy from when He first touched me on my hand seventy years ago."

"Benjamin!" yelled Leah as her grandfather's hand slowly pulled from hers and he fell from the bench onto the cool dirt floor.

Leah and Benjamin both jumped from the table to kneel beside him in the dirt.

What they saw not only shocked them, but touched them deeper than any emotion ever had before.

For not only was there no fear in the face of the old man, but his was a face of pure joy as he smiled from ear to ear.

With his trembling hands, he reached out for theirs. Once he held each of them, he looked first Benjamin in the eye and then settled on Leah.

"I am going home now, granddaughter. I am going home to be with Him for eternity. As I leave you now, I beg of you one last favor."

"Anything," answered Leah as tears fell freely from her eyes to land on her grandfather's smiling face. "Anything."

"Please," said her grandfather as he squeezed her hand with the last of his earthly strength. "Please tell my story. Please tell *His* story. Start tomorrow if you can. Don't repeat the mistake of a frightened old man. Show the strength and courage I lacked. But when you do tell my story, tell it with joy and pure faith. Because you are telling *His* story. When you tell this story, you will be spreading His light of goodness and helping to illuminate the path away from darkness and evil. Trust me on this. Have faith in Him and you will defeat the intent of the evil on this mortal world and stand with Him for eternity. Do this, and we will *both* see you in but the blink of an eye in Heaven."

The old man then slowly closed his eyes and exhaled his last breath on earth.

Leah leaned down and hugged her grandfather as tears of sorrow wracked her body. After several moments, Benjamin gently pulled her up by the shoulders.

"Do not be sad, my wife," said Benjamin as he pointed at the old man's face which still retained its smile of pure joy. "Be happy. I doubted more than most but now I am more certain than ever that what your grandfather said is true. I now believe that this man Jesus did walk among us over seventy years ago and is who your grandfather said he was. I feel it now. I suddenly feel that unexplained energy flowing through me."

Leah looked at her husband and now saw in his eyes, the same light that had been in her grandfather's eyes at the beginning of the night.

"My wife, before your grandfather began his story, I always believed myself to be a good man, a good husband, and a good father trying to do the right things. But to be honest, I always felt emptiness inside. As if a part of me had been missing since as long as I can remember. But I feel that emptiness no more. Suddenly, I feel whole and know what was missing which is now within me and makes me whole."

"What is that, my husband?"

Benjamin looked down at the smiling face of Leah's grandfather and then back into the eyes of the best person he had ever known.

"*Faith,* my dear wife. A purpose. I can't explain it but I now have complete faith that everything your grandfather just told us is true. I have faith in his story and more importantly, as one who spent a lifetime doubting, I now have complete faith in the story of this man Jesus and His message for us all. It is a message I will begin to spread tomorrow."

Leah then grabbed both of her husband's hands in hers as her eyes noticed that a new dawn was breaking outside.

"No, my husband…it is a message *we* will begin to spread… today. Starting with…"

Leah then looked over at her children who were starting to wake.

"…Hannah and Joseph. We will tell our own children first of this King of Kings. We will tell our children about Jesus and His message of love and salvation. And then, for the rest of our mortal lives, we will tell all who we meet of my grandfather's miraculous story. We will tell them of the man sent down by God to save us all. We will tell them *together,* my husband."

About the Author

D. Michael MacKinnon is a former White House and Pentagon official. While at the White House he had the high honor to write for two Presidents. Additionally, he has written for every major paper in the nation as well as appearing on all of the major television and cable networks as a political commentator. He is a bestselling author and novelist. Often homeless as a child, at five years of age a little plastic replica of the Baby Jesus touched him and changed his life forever.